BOUND

BOUND

KALIMAH WILLIAMS

PPW Publishing, LLC

To Aunt Brenda, who believed in me first. To Shella, for doing the heavy lifting. To Aunt Jo, for pushing me across the finish line. To Willie, this here our book, all soldiers have to die. To Ms. V, for the sweat, tears & Starbucks. To my Hype Team, no one does it better. If I ever forget who I am, I know where to find me.

PPW
PUBLISHING

Enjoy !
K. Williams

| 1 |

In the universe two figures meet, bathed in golden light. They are charged with a mission to lead and a path to keep.

"Racham, what do we do now?"

"We do what we have always done, Maveth. Is it not our purpose to do what the Master has commanded?"

He nodded his head in agreement but his caramel skin and fiery eyes glowed with righteous anger. "It is a slippery slope these humans travel upon. I will be glad when this is done. When we can all go home and do nothing but rejoice and languish in Him."

"Patience, my friend." Racham chuckled a little, making his intricately woven locs bob up and down his back. His deep amber eyes held compassion and tenderness in their gaze. His smooth dark cocoa face spoke of a boldness tempered in love. He too was ready for it to be done, but they had to see this through to the end. No shortcuts. They'd traveled through several decades, over countless miles and touched many lives in this process, all for this moment. They would not fail.

| 2 |

The boy lay broken and bruised in the back of the old pick-up truck. It was freezing. Every bump made the smell of urine, feces and blood waft up to his nose. His stomach lurched and retracted with the rhythm of the pick-up. A hard stop sent him flying into the side of the rusted bed face first, opening a fresh torrent of blood from his eye.

Two doors open and slam shut. A White face loomed over the boy; no recognizable features only a pale ghostly complexion.

"Son?"

Bishop Thomas shot up in bed, his heart racing and his breath coming fast and shallow. Sweat drenched his Egyptian cotton sheets making them sticky and inescapable. Thomas fought with the expensive fabric, his panic growing until he felt the cool air caress his left foot.

After scrambling from the bed Thomas wobbled to the master bathroom. He opened the cold tap full throttle and splashed water on his face. Still trying to recover, Thomas leaned back on one of the full length mirrors that lined the wall.

The memory was so strong Thomas shivered and held his breath against the stench from his nightmare. He felt like something was running into his eye but repeated wipes showed nothing on his hands. Thomas dropped down to the pristine marble tiled floor for a set of pushups. Up and down, up and down, wide arm and close hand with perfect form until his muscles shook with exhaustion. Overcome with fatigue, he collapsed on the floor, his sweat pooling into the grout. For a sixty-five year old man he was in better shape than most twenty year olds.

The physical strain helped him get his thoughts together. Being locked up could play games with your head. Thomas hadn't been bound to a 6x8 cell in over 15 years, but he still woke up in cold sweats thinking he was trapped back in the Mississippi State Penitentiary System. Twenty-three hours a day, alone, with no one but the person you hated the most to keep you company could end in disastrous results. If a man wasn't careful he could lose himself completely.

The time he'd spent in a cage forced him to condition his heart, head and body. When the new laws were put in place making it mandatory for prisoners to get exercise, education and religious freedoms, Thomas took full advantage. It was his beacon of light and he relished every moment.

During the day he lived in the prison library reading everything he could get his hands on. He consumed all the classics, The Art of War, War and Peace, The Grapes of Wrath, Animal Farm and The Bible. He absorbed knowledge like a sponge and eventually earned a Master's Degree in Psychology.

At night he was haunted by a burlap sack filled with money. The mental footage of that night played in his head on a constant loop. He went over every scenario, backwards and forwards, playing out multiple variations with the same ending, victory for him. If he'd only been bigger, smarter, faster, that night wouldn't have ended in him doing over two decades of hard time. He'd never seen that much money before and he was itching to get his hands on more than that when he got out.

Right now he was so close he could taste it. He'd worked on his God con in the big house and perfected it in churches and various houses of worship in the South. Any place he could get a baby toe in and a nickel out, he told his story of the poor misguided boy who reached his hands out in worship to a God who'd blessed him with forgiveness and a second chance to redeem himself. If the secret weapon of a long con was half-truths then its enemy was over embellishment. Thomas was always honest about the time he'd spent incarcerated. People ate up the juicy stories of sin and self-indulgence, especially ones filled with moral corruption and secrets.

Living Waters had been a good stopping place for him. Thomas had built a reputation on the road as a traveling preacher, but Living Waters afforded him the opportunity to build relationships and trust. A way to put aside the snatch and grab revivals that guest speaking afforded him and get into some serious cash flow with little effort and lots of finesse. In twenty-four hours he'd have everything he needed to start his new life.

Just as quickly as he dropped to the ground Thomas jumped back up again. Today of all days was not the day to be lying around. He took a quick shower, invested some considerable time on his daily hygiene routine, dressed in his typical khakis, polo, sports coat combo and entered the adjoining upstairs office.

Thomas sat behind his desk in a plush, self-heating leather chair and smiled at the breakfast tray and morning paper Eugenia had laid out for him. He took the time to rub his hand over the fine grain of the Gabon Ebony wood. *It's a shame,* he lamented, as he thought about how much it was going to cost him to replace the costly furniture he'd procured from a high profile judge at a high stakes poker game.

He didn't have to lift the silver domed top on his plate to know what was underneath. There were always two eggs over easy, three crisp pieces of bacon, four slivers of tomato and half a cup of sliced strawberries, blueberries and bananas. Prison had also made him a creature of habit. It was easier to concentrate on and anticipate the outside influences of a project when he kept a routine.

Eugenia had serviced him for the last five years. Replacing her, when he got to his new location, would be an essential and arduous task. The hefty severance pay he'd give her, in cash, would ensure her silence. If it didn't, there were ways to close an open mouth with a loose tongue. Prison had also allowed him to meet new acquaintances with different criminal skill sets than his. This morning's meal was the last official duty she would perform. She would be instructed to find a permanent place of relocation for her family and never speak of her employment with him.

Thomas used the multi-device remote control to turn on the 72-inch flat screen wall mounted television.

"Good Morning Georgia. I'm Tracy Phillips from WJKZ Channel 6 News, your prime source for what's happening in your neighborhood. There is a developing story this morning..."

He lowered the volume not wanting his breakfast to be interrupted by any unsavory reports of murder and mayhem. Tracy Phillips was one of his favorite anchors, more for her looks than her skill, but he wasn't in the mood for any eye candy this morning.

What he really wanted to do was check the offshore account, but it wasn't time yet. Now, it was time for breakfast. He ate in relative silence, daydreaming about island life. No more a pauper, in the Philippines he would be a prince. Maybe even an emperor with the money he'd siphoned over the years added to his big score.

The group of small islands, with their high populations and multicultural backgrounds, was an ideal place for Thomas to disappear. The fact that they had no extradition treaty with the United States was like adding a cherry on top of an already fully loaded sundae. The end was in sight, all he had to do was keep a cool head and hold tight.

His meal complete and his fantasies soon to be fulfilled, he was finally able to move on with the rest of his day. Thomas opened one of his top drawers and pulled out a stiff plastic accordion portfolio. He took his time unraveling the cotton string that secured the folder. The unwinding heightened his anticipation and excitement. He felt the front of his pants tighten as he reached inside and fondled his passport and plane ticket for the unpteenth time.

Magandang umaga maganda. Good morning beautiful. Thomas practiced the Tagalog phrase until it rolled off his tongue. He mused that was all he'd need to know when he landed. His charm and good looks would carry him the rest of the way. Women weren't a priority for Thomas while he was working. Divided attentions made for messy work and a neglect of the small details. The fairer species were hell on a routine; you never knew when they might want to surprise you with some grand expression of their love.

No, it was easier to work alone. You could reap all the benefits of your own reward. None of that would matter in the Philippines. He'd have so many women he could change them daily and wear them like suits if he wanted to.

The vibration from Thomas's cell phone made it float across the desk by a few millimeters. He quickly scanned the screen and saw that it was only Dominic Trippler calling him. *I wonder what he wants. Probably checking to make sure his withdrawal is set for the 15th.*

Dominic always got jumpy a few days before his contribution was taken out of his checking account. Thomas chuckled to himself when he thought about the angst he'd feel when he saw the withdrawal had been made five days ahead of schedule and for ten times the amount. It didn't make any difference. The last of the transactions should have come through first thing this morning.

Thomas entered the web address for the international bank. The phone began to vibrate again, this time skipping across the desk from the force of the vibrations. He disregarded the screen, pushing the ignore button instead. Anxiously, he typed in his login name and password. His phone started vibrating again, this time falling off the desk. He picked it up irritated by its incessant movement, and threw it in the middle slide drawer of the desk.

Poising his finger over the 'enter' key Thomas closed his eyes savoring the moment. In one second all of his hard work would have paid off, but his phone would not let up. It banged up against the hard interior of the drawer and its contents, trying to knock itself free of its fine wooden box. His moment ruined, Thomas pressed the enter key unceremoniously. Tears welled up in the corner of his eyes; his throat became dry and swollen with emotion and he began to hyperventilate when he saw the bright red warning.

FROZEN.

"Shit!"

| 3 |

Maveth stood behind Bishop Thomas, a slow smile spreading across his face. He avoided looking at Racham so he could enjoy his mirth in peace.

"Maveth", Racham admonished him with the sharp call of his name. "Gloating is not an attribute of our Master."

"Gloating? You mis-read me brother. The source of my joy is not this human's downfall. In fact, I am saddened he has squandered every opportunity given him to repent."

"Saddened?" Racham questioned?

"Yes, brother. Deeply." Maveth countered.

"My apologies, brother. I have misjudged you. Perhaps you should also inform your face, it appears as if it is also unaware of your deep sadness."

"I am, at times, misunderstood."

"Come, Maveth. Events have been set into motion. We must be in place."

| 4 |

"Hello and good afternoon Georgia. I'm Tracy Phillips from WJKZ Channel 6 News, your prime source for what's happening in your neighborhood. We interrupt your currently scheduled program to bring you late breaking news. Police are searching for Junior Pastor Damian Hardwin of Living Waters Congregation in Lakefield, Georgia. The young zealous pastor, a church favorite, who is said to have renewed Living Waters' membership to almost double in the past three years, is being sought on felony embezzlement and fraud charges. All of WJKZ's attempts to reach Senior Pastor Mario Fellows have yet to garner any response."

* * *

Pastor Mario Fellows sat in his leather reclining chair watching the local news and couldn't believe what he was hearing. A paralyzing chill ran down his spine. The sour taste of guilt was lodged deep in the back of his throat. No wonder his telephone had been ringing off the hook.

"How could this happen?"

Fellows looked at the caller ID on the phone and turned the TV down.

"This is the last person I want to speak to". He took a sip of courage from his warmed beer, and answered the phone reluctantly.

"Hello? Yes I'm watching it now. No, Mother Wilson, I don't know. Yes, Mother Wilson, if I...The church hasn't...It's the first...Look, I have to go." He muttered before hanging up the phone.

"That nosy old biddy is always looking for some gossip," Mario felt bad about his outburst and half-heartedly added a, "Lord, forgive me, all of this is my fault."

Pastor Fellows sat back in his recliner, increased the volume on the TV, turned up his half empty beer can and watched his life disintegrate in one gulp.

| 5 |

"Authorities were made aware of the alleged crime when Dominic and Patricia Trippler received a call from their bank requesting authorization for a $100,000 wire transfer to an overseas bank account for a non-profit organization they'd been making contributions towards. After trying, unsuccessfully, to contact Bishop Anthony Thomas, the Tripplers began calling around to the other members of their "mission circle". The "mission circle" was a program set up under the direction of Junior Pastor Damian Hardwin, with a small elite group of Living Waters' wealthiest members as its patrons. Members were sold on the principles of discipleship and spreading the word of God to the far corners of some of the world's poorer communities. Thomas is said to have cited jealousy as the reason they could not spread the news of the circle's good works.

Members of the circle had reportedly written several checks over the past year for $10,000. However, they were all shocked when they found that their bank accounts had been accessed without their permission, through a series of electronic transfers, all within the last 72 hours. Of the ten couples involved in the scam only two escaped the $100,000 fleecing due to extensive security measures at their individual banks. Police are currently searching for Bishop Anthony Thomas, the alleged accomplice of Pastor Hardwin. Hardwin is said to be the money man in what investigators are now dubbing the 'Circle Scam'. A federal investigative team has traced a minimum of three overseas accounts to Pastor Hardwin. We'll bring you more of this devastating story as it unfolds.

For now I'm Tracy Phillips WJKZ bringing you the news in your neighbor-hood. We now return you to your regularly scheduled program."

| 6 |

Damian Hardwin stared at his TV with his mouth agape, his chin cradled between his left thumb and forefinger. He could see the lips moving on the Channel 6 news reporter, but his brain was struggling to catch up with her words. *"...a minimum of three overseas accounts to Pastor Hardwin"*, snapped Damian out of his self induced trance and set him in motion.

"Damn, I knew he would get too greedy. How stupid could he be? Everything is gonna fall back on me. I should've listened to Shonen from day one." Damian muttered to himself as he passed from the closet to the bed where he was trying to stuff as much of his clothes and shoes as he could fit into three large black duffel bags. Damian's stomach bubbled at the thought of getting caught before he could make his getaway.

If he hadn't had so much on his plate he would've figured it out sooner. The manila folder marked Dream Catcher moved over, around, on the bottom of and on the top of multiple to do stacks of work on his desk for two months before Damian found a quiet minute to flip through its contents. He'd been dealing with one headache after the other and needed something to lift his spirits. On a whim he picked up the folder and searched for a phone number to call so he could check on the needy faces staring up at him on the glossy brochure.

After several transfers he was able to speak to a man named Juan Rivera. Mr. Rivera in a mixture of broken English and slurred Spanish explained to him that he was the one to answer telefono. Frustrated with the futile communication Mr. Rivera answered one last question for Damian before he hung up the phone. Damian's Spanish wasn't the best but he was sure that discoteca did not translate into orphanage or school.

Damian was livid. Thomas lied straight to his face with no hesitation. He'd been duped, Living Waters would be mired in scandal, Pastor Fellows and Shonen along with the rest of the Board were going to kill him.

Anger drove him from his office. The distinct gruffness of Thomas' deep baritone voice acted as a homing beacon guiding him to his target. He turned the corner to see Thomas holding court with Linda Prentiss and Joe Wilson. Damian stood in the hallway with the manila folder held high over his head and let his fury announce his presence.

Linda was the first to feel Damian's rage. Its forcefulness choked off her conversation before it caused Joe to turn and gawk at him. Thomas felt it too, but he was enjoying his offensive position. He let Damian stew a little before turning to act like he had no idea he'd been standing there.

"Pastor Hardwin, good to see you. How has the Almighty bestowed favor on His most faithful servant this afternoon?"

Thomas grinned like a psychotic cat playing with his prey. Damian wanted to plow his fist into Thomas's mouth and break every grinder, molar and incisor that dared to mock him.

"My. Office. Now." Damian squeezed out through a tightly clenched jaw before marching back to his office.

Linda placed a hand on Thomas's arm, halting him. "Is everything ok?"

"God willing and the creek don't rise. I'm sure it's nothing, probably a little misunderstanding. You know these youngsters; they get all excited for no reason. Then, when you drop a little knowledge on them, they simmer down." Thomas patted Linda's hand and politely removed it from his bicep.

Joe wanted to participate in the drama but he wasn't sure how to insert himself. His mother's voice was screaming in his head, *This is why they keep passing you over for the Board, you never show any initiative. You get that cowardly spirit from your Daddy's side of the family. No initiative in you at all."* He did the only thing he could think of to show his solidarity with Bishop Thomas.

"You want me to call Mother? Get the Prayer Warriors to lift you up in prayer?"

"I'm sure it's not a big enough stink to get the Prayer Warriors involved but I could always use a good God fearing woman like Mother Wilson on my side." Thomas winked at Joe knowingly and then went to Damian.

"Knock, knock," Thomas called out jovially, stopping short of the threshold.

"Come in and close the door," Damian barked, standing up from his chair and walking around to the front of his desk.

"Your wish is my command Pastor." Thomas came in and closed the door slowly. He elongated every action purposely trying to push Damian to the edge of his patience.

"Cut the crap Thomas." Damian jabbed his finger on the folder. "Explain this."

"Did you speak to Mr. Rivera?"

"Yes?" Damian was confused. Thomas's question made him stagger mentally.

"Then why are you asking me dumb ass questions young buck?" Bishop Thomas asked, dropping his holy façade. He felt like Atlas without the burden of the world on his shoulders.

"Did you-"

"Yes the hell I did. You heard me patna! Since, you're sitting there with that goofy ass look on your face, I'll break it down for you, cuz you look confused. Ha! All that book sense and you lack the most important thing in life you need, common sense."

The wheels in Damian's brain were beginning to turn.

"You set me up?" The statement came out like a question. Damian couldn't point out the nuances or connect all the dots, but he knew from the smug look on Thomas's face that all roads would lead to his front door.

"No. You set yourself up by not paying attention. Have a seat son."

Damian stood his ground.

"I said have a seat son."

Damian refused to move.

"I tell you what. Keep standing," Thomas strode over to Damian's desk and picked the phone up out of its cradle before he finished his threat. "I'll just call Mario and Shonen and explain to them about the discrepancies I've found in the bookkeeping. This phone does allow you to use three way with the intercom on, doesn't it?"

Damian sat down in one of the chairs he normally reserved for guests.

"Now let me explain to you why you're going to keep your mouth shut and stay out of my way."

| 7 |

Racham and Maveth were watching over a sleeping Janice. She rolled back and forth on the queen sized bed, thrashing and fighting with an invisible enemy.

"Shh...", Racham comforted. He sat on the bed and rubbed his big hand over her hair and back. Janice immediately stopped moving and settled into a peaceful sleep.

"You have always held a soft spot for this one."

Racham rose at the accusation and repositioned himself beside Maveth. "I carry a soft spot for all of humanity."

"No, you carry compassion for all humanity. This one has burrowed underneath your skin and you carry her there." Maveth poked a finger into Racham's chest where his heart would be.

Racham wanted to object, but the flare of Maveth's nostrils and quick leap of fire in his eyes was a caution to tread lightly with any mistruth. "I do not know if what I carry for her is a soft spot. What I am sure of is that her little life has given me nightmares."

"You and I have roamed this earth for more years than I care to recall. We have seen tragedy, depravity, and all manner of sin in these humans. How is she any different?"

"She was a child. A child we were not allowed to comfort." Racham waved off Maveth's objections. "I know, I know. There are many, too many children, as well. Perhaps therein lies my soft spot. She is one of many. There were many before her, there have been many after her and there will be many more to come. It is...tiring."

Maveth shook his head before answering, "Complete the task, so we can go."

Racham bent down slowly and whispered in Janice's ear before evaporating into the night.

| 8 |

One Year Ago

Janice woke up feeling inspired. She'd tossed and turned for hours before dropping off into a deep sleep. In her dream the mattress turned into a cloud. She sunk down into the pillowy, cotton candy like spheres, and had the most peaceful sleep.

She went about her Sunday morning rituals, getting ready for Bedside Baptist, when she noticed a buzzing sound in the back of her head that she couldn't get rid of. The more she tried to distract herself from it, the louder it became. Janice made her way into the bathroom to take some headache powder, under normal circumstances it always did the trick. This time, there was no immediate rush of relief and the buzzing moved from the back of her brain to the front.

The sudden change made her feel nauseous and dizzy. Janice grabbed onto the sink to steady herself. The buzzing was replaced by a voice that was familiar, but incoherent. The words repeated themselves over and over, louder and louder, until they slammed into her brain, like a sledgehammer.

"Go...To...Him."

As soon as she heard the words, she knew exactly what they meant. They'd told her to get ready. She'd done the work, but she still didn't feel worthy.

Janice hadn't missed a meeting. She attended every week, faithfully. Even when she felt weak she popped in on wherever one was being held. The half-way house where she puked her guts out, the first 72 hours of her recovery, upgraded her from client to employee. Her sponsor had even recommended she sponsor other addicts because she had worked her program so well.

A program designed to help reacclimate addicts back into society helped Janice get her teeth fixed, an Associate's Degree in Social Work and get settled into a new house. All of it had been in preparation for this day.

They came to her four years ago when she was at her lowest. She hadn't seen her son since he was a little boy. Their meeting wasn't one she liked to remember, but it was one she couldn't afford to forget.

* * *

Janice was on the hunt when she saw him. She almost passed him up because he didn't have the look to meet her immediate needs. It had been a long while since Janice could set up a "date" to get her enough money to get a fix. Lately, she had to rob, beg or borrow. Nobody on God's green earth was going to let her borrow anything. She'd already tried her hand at robbery that morning. Her swollen-blackened eye was proof of how disastrous that had been. Begging was her least favorite option and would be the hardest to make a come up on. Janice needed to find her a sweet spot sucker, somebody centrally located between pity and save-a-ho.

The two men she saw coming out of The Breakfast Nookery, laughing and joking with each other, were too entranced with each other to pay her any mind. They looked "churchy". Those types wanted to pray for you, invite you to their church and take a picture helping you so they could post it on Facebook for the world to see how charitable they were. They never had any real cash on them. It wasn't worth Janice's time trying to get blood from those two turnips. She was hot, tired and wanted to get high before the fifth of vodka she chugged that morning wore off.

They were mostly a second thought when the tall one with the smooth mahogany skin turned his head and Janice saw the scar. She inched closer to the men to get a better look. Before she could catch herself, words were tumbling out of her mouth.

"Man-Man?" she whisper-questioned in a small voice. "Man-Man," she whispered, louder, with force, and beckoned him closer.

Janice knew she looked bad, knew she smelled bad too. The vomit stained multi-color wig she wore was making her dizzy from the fumes wafting around her. She wore a Clippers jersey mini-dress with stains forensic files couldn't sort through. Still, the look in his eyes held a disgust that went beyond the physical embodiment in front of him.

Something in the pit of her stomach felt like it was on the long ascent of the world's tallest, loopiest roller coaster. Janice hated roller coasters, ever since she was a young girl. The starts, stops, teetering and plummets were more than she could ever handle or enjoy.

"Damian, come on man, let's go."

Damian. That was his name. Cara gave it to him, she always hated it. Janice cut her eyes at the man rushing Man-Man.

"Hold up man, I'm coming. Let me see what this sister needs."

"What this sister need? Boy, you funny! Ha-ha, why you act like you don't know me boy?"

"I'm sorry ma'am; there's been a misunderstanding, some sort of mistake. I've never seen you before. I can see you're sick though. Would you like me to...pray for you?"

"Nigga, pray? Pray? You sound like ya gotdamn daddy."

"My daddy? Look lady, I don't know who you think I am. I don't know who you think you are. I don't even know my daddy. That's a secret that died with my momma thirty years ago."

"D man, come on!"

Damian threw his hand up to his friend in frustration. "I said hold up!"

"Ma'am, I'd really like to pray for you. Maybe get you a bite to eat? Would you like that?"

Who the fuck did he think he was, Janice thought. She walked around Damian in slow circles, examining him up and down, shaking her head in agreement with herself.

"Yep, yep, nigga, that's you. Look just like that preacher man too." *Hell, he was the only one I really remember. Climbed on these thighs like he was about to deliver the Sermon on the Mount.*

Irritated he didn't immediately respond, Janice rolled her eyes. "Man-Man? It's me, your momma, Janice."

"Janice? My..." Damian let his words hang in the air.

"Yeah boy. Your momma. You standing here talkin' 'bout 'my momma dead'. Do I look dead to you? Smell bad, but dead, uh uh. 'Sides if I was dead I couldn't get high could I? Nope."

"My mother is dead." Damian didn't sound convincing.

"You look smart." Janice said sarcastically, stalking him in a drunken semi-circle again. "But you a little slow on the uptake. I'M YO MOMMA! Damn. You wanna see your name on my stretch marks, nigga? Who told you I was dead?"

"I can't-" Damian sputtered.

"It don't matter. It don't matter. It was that bitch Cara won't it?" Janice accused, pointing her finger in Damian's face.

"Aunt Cara?"

"Yeah, I knew it was her. Mad cause I got seven kids. Always trying to tell somebody how to raise what she ain't got. That bitch uterus is what's dead, not me." *Fuck her and fuck him too if he thought he was gonna stand in the street and act like he don't know his own momma.*

All Damian could offer her was a blank stare.

"Oh, I see what it is now. You lookin' at me with that stupid ass look on your face. Cara got you thinking you better than me?" Janice could feel her sanity slipping away. "Y'all sittin' up in the house talkin' shit 'bout me?"

"Lady-"

"Don't lady me, like I aint nobody." Janice hit her fist on her chest for emphasis. "I'm yo MOMMA!"

"Listen, I don't know what your game is but I'm going to tell you for the last time MY MOMMA IS DEAD." Damian exclaimed through clenched teeth. He dug his wallet out of his back pants pocket, took a hundred dollar bill out of his wallet and shoved it into Janice's hands. "Is this what you want? Is this what you're looking for? Here, take this and leave me alone, forever!"

Janice didn't want to take the money. The more Damian shoved and pushed the crisp bill into her hand the weaker her muscles became, until she was holding onto the money for dear life. Need and shame warred inside her. Janice made two promises to herself as she watched Damian stomp away from her; 1) Damian would be her last trick and 2) she was going to take the money he gave her and ride one last hit into oblivion.

* * *

Janice was so preoccupied with her heartache that day, she didn't realize she was being followed. She was halfway through her stash and well into her journey to the upper room when they came to her. They promised to save her with the condition that she be obedient when they returned.

There wasn't anything she wouldn't have promised to make the pain go away. The salvation they offered her was different. For the first time, in a long time, Janice felt at peace within herself. The hateful voices that haunted her were quiet. She slept and rested; worked her plan, fasted and prayed, all in an effort to be ready when the time came.

Now that peace was being replaced with a fluttering inside her stomach. She made a deal and a promise, it was time to pay up and follow through. Janice put on her best dress, put the address to Living Waters into the GPS on her phone, said a quick prayer and headed out to reacquaint herself with her son.

| 9 |

Damian found himself overwhelmed by church members about a year ago. Pastor Fellows was going through some hard times and had all but thrown the time consuming responsibilities of Living Waters into his lap. Being an attractive single Black man made the situation that much worse. Never a stranger to the attention of women, Damian thought the ones who'd dedicated themselves to God would have a clearer focus and not fawn over the looks he'd been blessed with and the body he worked hard for. They even loved the ugliest part of him. A scar he'd gotten as a baby ran from the outside corner of his right eye down his cheek. They thought it made him look rugged and masculine and they weren't shy about letting him know it.

The truth was they were the worst. They found all sorts of church business, in all manner of dress or undress, to speak to him about. A few of them had even shown up at his door begging for a late night session of counseling. When he'd come home late one evening to find a woman had been bold enough to break into his place to cook dinner for them and arrange herself suggestively on his bed, all under the guise of God telling her that she'd been sent to take care of him, he knew the situation had gotten out of control.

Lucky for him nobody knew about his safe house but him and her. Not even Bishop Thomas, his assumed partner in crime, knew that he'd leased this tiny apartment under his mother's name. To anyone who asked, she'd died a long time ago. It wasn't the truth but it helped to alleviate any questions about his upbringing. Unfortunately, he'd learned the lies you create to make your life easier are the same ones that resurface to wreck the havoc in your life you were trying to avoid.

* * *

He was greeting visitors and guests, when an attractive older woman approached him after second service. She looked familiar to him, but he couldn't quite place her, until she called his name. What his eyes failed to see, his heart leapt to acknowledge.

"Damian?"

He stared in disbelief. The woman standing before him was shapely, well-manicured and clean. She wore a peach short tuxedo cut jacket over a simple ivory dress, with gold accents. Damian was reminded of a picture his Aunt Cara used to show him growing up of a young girl whose face lit up the entire photograph. He remembered studying it for hours, daydreaming about those eyes and that smile looking down on him while she rocked him to sleep.

"Janice?"

"In the flesh," she answered flippantly. One look at the expression on Damian's face and Janice knew her attempt at levity had failed.

Damian opened his mouth to make an excuse, before walking away from her. She anticipated his unwillingness to chat and cut him off.

"Wait." Janice said, reaching out to him. "I don't want to make a scene. Please, can I talk to you for a moment?"

His eyes slid to the ground as he contemplated her request. After a few deep breaths, Damian relented.

"A moment and that's it."

"Is there somewhere private we can go?"

"With you?" Damian scoffed. "Why would I go anywhere private with you?"

"I just want to talk son."

"Son? Only a mother could call me that."

Janice hung her head in shame, she prayed silently, asking God to soften Damian's heart against her. Her sponsor told her this part of recovery wouldn't be easy. She'd warned her people she'd hurt would want retaliation before they'd want reconciliation.

"Damian. I'm sorry, truly sorry. I can't make up for any of it, but if you let-"

"Fine. There's a coffee shop across the street, let me get my things. Get a table and I'll meet you there."

"Thank-you." Janice took the compromise with gratitude and hurried across the street before Damian could change his mind.

| 10 |

Damian took his time gathering his things. His office was sparse and there wasn't much to gather other than his thoughts and feelings. Unlike his office, they were all over the place. No amount of drawer opening and closing was going to make her go away, and he was running out of items to rearrange on his desk. Damian locked his door and began the trek down the long hallway of Living Waters' administrative offices. The forest green carpet might as well have been made of sifting sand, the way Damian's feet plodded along. The last time he saw Janice had been a disaster.

He prayed he would never see her again. His life was complicated enough without adding Janice to the mix. Every day he asked God to help him fight his demons, his temptations and his weaknesses. Lately, it seemed like He was unmoved by his pleas.

Damian stopped outside his mentors office. He gave the door a few short timid knocks before remembering that Pastor Fellows wasn't there. He missed the older man's wise counsel. Fellows had been missing in action for too long.

Most people didn't realize how long Fellows had actually been gone. Damian covered for his mentor, knowing he'd had a hard time adjusting to his involuntary foray into single life. Initially, they spoke every few days. Then every couple of weeks until they're check-ins became monthly terse exchanges.

Damian didn't offer a lot of information and Fellows didn't ask. He left Damian to his own devices, letting him make all of the important decisions by himself. Damian was hurt and confused. This was one instance the young minister didn't want to be alone. He thought about calling Shonen, but his pride and lies made reaching out to him an idea he quickly discarded.

| 11 |

The strong aroma of Columbian Roast caressed Damian's senses as soon as he walked through the door of the small cafe. He took a moment to breathe in the nutty, buttery smell accented with notes of caramel and vanilla.

"Can I get a Large Columbian, please?"

"Sure sir. Large Columbian." The overly cheerful cashier yelled absently over his shoulder, speaking directly to no one.

Damian watched with amusement as multiple hands worked in unison to produce one cup of coffee. He wished he could apply their skills to deal with Janice. A whole assembly line to help him compartmentalize the anger, love, frustration, longing and pain he felt when he thought about *her*. Just thinking about it was overwhelming.

"That'll be one dollar and eighty-three cents.", announced the cashier, placing the strong brew in front of Damian.

Damian dug into his pants pocket and fished out some loose change, handing it over without counting out the exact amount.

"Oh, looks like you gave me too much, sir. This is, let me see, one dollar and ninety-nine cents."

The cashier's faux friendliness was beginning to grate on Damian's nerves.

"Keep the change." Damian replied.

"Literally!" the cashier beamed.

Damian eyed the cashier over the rim of his cup. He took a long pull of the seductive elixir and let it warm his chest. When he was certain the coffee would stay in his cup and not end up splattered all over the burnt orange apron of the cashier, Damian lowered his cup and gave the cashier a curt thanks.

Janice jumped up from her seat like a hyperactive puppy waiting on its master when she spotted Damian. She'd selected an intimate two-top in the far corner of the cafe and waved her hands wildly over her head signaling him to come over.

"I'm so glad you came. I thought you'd changed your mind. Sit, sit."

Damian resisted the urge to release an audible sigh. *One meeting without her embarrassing me is all I ask.* He sat down and immediately got to business.

"I don't have a lot of time."

"I know, I won't be long, promise."

Tears that previously pooled in the bottom folds of Janice's eyes now ran freely down her cheeks. They made big splashes on the front of her ivory dress, giving the thin fabric a faux look of transparency. She opened her hands to welcome one of his but Damian kept his hands wrapped around the steaming cup of rich coffee, silently declining her offer.

Staying angry with her was proving to be hard work. Damian felt his posture relax and his countenance melt with her tears. A part of him wanted God to take over and allow him to forgive her completely. The other part wanted her to pay and hurt as bad as he had.

His Aunt Cara had been a good mother to him, but *her* picture had haunted him. The days and nights he'd spent longing for her felt fresh in this moment and he hated her for it. Raw emotion swelled in his chest, pressing against his rib cage, threatening to spill out and destroy everything in its path.

Damian hung his head, willing the storm inside him to subside. The grief of a childhood lost and the bitterness of an unfulfilled longing pissed him off even more. When he raised his head to look at the woman who'd abandoned him every hurt, real and imagined, drilled into her spirit through his eyes. Contempt seeped from his pores. The coldness he felt towards her made Janice visibly shiver.

"I'm sorry."

"You've said that already," Damian said through clenched teeth. He dragged one massive hand across his face trying to crush the demons of revenge and disregard warring inside him.

Janice cleared her throat and tried again. "I don't know exactly what to say," she confessed.

Damian stared at her with flat, passionless eyes. The storm was over but what had been left in its wake was a vacuum of emptiness. Unable to fully trust or control his emotions, he made himself void of everything.

"You're the only one I could find," she began. "I don't know what happened to the others."

Damian sipped his cooling coffee and raised his left eyebrow in interest.

"You were the last one, the baby."

Leaning back in his chair, Damian continued to drink but gave no words to signal disgust or encouragement. Janice chose to interpret his silence as the latter and continued with her disjointed story.

"She found me by accident." Damian looked at Janice quizzically, brows furrowed, still confused with where the conversation was going. "Cara, I mean."

Janice's heart sank. All week she'd fasted and prayed about what to say to Damian if he agreed to speak with her. She didn't want him to look at her with anymore disgust. She felt her old self clawing its way to the surface. After all, none of this was completely her fault. She was as much of a victim as her baby boy was.

Janice licked her lips and felt the heat from a warm crack pipe tickle the tip of her tongue. When the familiar taste of crack stroked her tonsils she knew her thoughts had gone too deep into its old well. Outwardly, she shook her head, trying to free herself from her toxic thoughts. Inwardly, she recited the Serenity Prayer until she felt the need for a quick hit dissipate.

"I was whoring on 52nd and Sycamore. You know, over by the Rent-a-Bed Motel and Pee-Wee's, that chicken spot across the street next to the liquor store?"

Damian knew the corner well. Living Water had done some outreach programs in the area, trying to get The Lost a way to The Truth. The thought of him serving a cup of coffee to his own mother and witnessing to her without knowing was more than he could genuinely wrap his mind around.

He searched his memory bank for any impression of her. When the battered women's faces started to mix in with the images of stilettos, booty cutters, fishnets and lacy bras Damian gave up. There was no way he'd ever be able to recall such a miniscule moment in time.

"I know the spot. What about it?"

"I was with a trick." Janice interrupted her tale to question Damian. "You know what that is?"

Damian exhaled noisily. "Janice!"

"Ok, ok. I was just making sure. Anyway, I was with this trick and your Aunt Cara knocked on the driver side window of the backseat."

"I know I'm going to regret asking you," Damian professed, "but why was Aunt Cara knocking on the window of a car you were hoeing in?"

Janice cringed at Damian's casual utterance of her former profession, but she had no choice except to continue what she started. She shrugged when she answered, "Because I was in the backseat of your Uncle Earl's Cadillac."

The swig of coffee he'd taken skipped lanes, ignored the one way breathing sign and traveled down into his trachea. Damian held onto the table, steadying himself through the spasms in his lungs as they struggled to receive oxygen. His eyes watered and snot spewed from his nostrils.

"Damian, breathe!" Janice jumped up screaming, pounding him on his back.

Damian cocked his head to the side and looked up at Janice in disbelief. As if his choking were something he'd made a conscious decision to do. He used his other hand to loosen his silk purple tie and undo the top button of his dress shirt.

Panicked, Janice grabbed his left wrist and jerked his arm above his head. Damian tried to pull his arm out of her grip. The harder he resisted, the more she pulled. Fighting her only made it worse. Damian, spitting and sputtering, finally gave in to Janice's tugging and slapping.

Janice rubbed Damian's back, wanting to sooth him as his choking subsided. Her efforts were wasted. When Damian was able to regain his composure he knocked her hand off. If the hard look he gave her was any indicator, his near death experience hadn't softened his thoughts towards her.

Janice waited. Damian moved his hand in a rolling motion prompting her to continue.

"It wasn't like that with me and Earl. I didn't know he was Cara's husband. I hadn't had any contact with any of my sisters for years. The last time we'd all gotten together was for Ma Lou's funeral, some ten odd years before."

"Ma Lou? I think I remember Aunt Cara mentioning her a few times."

"I can't imagine it was in conjunction with anything nice." Janice's lips curled with malice.

Her look made Damian want to know more.

"Who was she?"

Janice shook her head. She felt the tears again, burning against her eyelids. Her head began to ache from the pressure building behind them.

"I don't want to talk about her," she murmured.

"Then I'm leaving." Damian stood to go. Janice placed her hand on his, halting his momentum.

"Wait."

Something about the way her voice broke when she asked him to stay made the glacier around his heart begin to melt. Damian squatted beside the table, balancing himself on the balls of his feet.

"This won't be easy." Searching her face for some commonality, he explained, "I'm angry and I'm hurt, but if you're willing to share with me, I'll share with you.

Janice took advantage of his closeness to rub the top of his head and kiss it gently. Damian wasn't comfortable with the gesture but if it got him the information he needed he would tolerate it.

"Okay, I'll tell you," she relented.

Damian stood up slowly, wincing at the pain in his right knee.

"You ok?"

"I'm fine, just an old football injury acting up."

Janice winked at him mischievously. "Go Templeton Tigers! 15-2 your senior season. Best running back two years in a row. Heisman trophy nominee."

The quick puff of Damian's chest signaled his pride and surprise. Her facts weren't completely correct, but she knew something. "Three."

"Three?"

"I was voted best All-American College Running Back three years in a row."

"Oh. My bad. I was high. That doesn't make for a good memory."

"And we're back," Damian stated, dryly.

"Sorry." Janice apologized for the quick change of subject. "My sponsor says I have an issue with filters and tact. It's common for long time addicts. It's like we've been living in our own heads for so long, making up the rules in our own worlds that we have a hard time adjusting to normal people etiquette."

"It's a little unsettling."

"I know, like ripping off a band-aid. Other people don't get it. It makes them uncomfortable. Addicts either clam-up or only talk to other addicts. Before you know it, you and your 'friend' are sharing a bump or a needle before NA meetings."

"Well," Damian sat back in his chair, trying to look more relaxed than he felt, "let the ripping commence. Who was Ma Lou?"

"She ran the local colored whore house. I was one of her best gals." Janice paused for a moment. Knowing the last piece of the puzzle always made her desire for crack a little sharper. The taste was back in her throat again, making her mouth water. She had to fight it. She'd been telling her story over and over again for months. It was supposed to get easier with each telling, but Janice had yet to find any relief.

"She was my mother."

| 12 |

Damian let the revelation wash over him. "Whoa."

"She sold us for pennies on the dollar, simply for the pleasure of doing so. We were poor, barely enough food to feed the rats and roaches that lived with us. The men fed us and in exchange they gave her a few dollars for her snuff and beer."

"Snuff and beer?"

Lost in her own recollections, Janice continued without any thought to Damian's inquiry, pushing away hot tears with the back of her hand.

"Nobody ever did anything?"

"Who was going to do anything?" Janice questioned indignantly. "Who cared about a few nappy headed whores? They took what they could get and left us to die!"

Damian didn't know what to do with her anger. He had the urge to hug her and tell her everything would be alright. He never knew about their childhood, he'd never cared. Aunt Cara always hushed him when he asked too many questions about his mother and their past. He'd assumed she was trying to spare him, not her.

"It's ok. It's ok."

"No, it's not."

"I know. Look, we don't have to talk about this anymore."

"No!" Janice cried. "You said, 'if I share you'll share'. I won't let them silence me anymore. I won't let them keep me from you anymore."

Confused, Damian succumbed to her request. "We'll keep going then. But, if you feel like you want to stop, that's okay too."

Resigned to her story, Janice continued. "Like I was saying before, the last time I'd seen Cara and the others was at Ma Lou's funeral. I think we all showed up to see if she was actually dead."

"So you all got a chance to hang out and catch up?" Damian asked, trying to lighten the mood.

"Naw. What's there to catch up on? What were we going to talk about, who fetched the highest price?"

Damian decided to try another tactic. "How many of you were there?"

"Six in all. Come to think of it," Janice thought out loud, "there were only four of us there for the funeral. Ruth Ann and Macie didn't make it."

"What happened to them? Why couldn't they make it?"

"I didn't say they couldn't make it. I said they didn't make it."

"I don't get it."

The craving snuck back in. Janice shook off the memory of Ma Lou's funeral and the faces of her sisters that tormented her.

"Macie died in a home. When Ma Lou got too old and sick the state took her. I was the baby, but I don't ever remember her talking or doing anything normal like the rest of us."

"And Ruth Ann?"

"Dead too. Murdered, they found her in a back alley with her throat cut. Ruth Ann was a bit of a daredevil. She'd go with anybody, never had the sense the streets should've taught her."

"Did Ma Lou make all of you-?" Damian let the question hang in the air.

"Every single one of us."

"Aunt Cara?"

"She was the oldest, and the favorite until I came along."

"Macie?"

Janice chuckled cynically, "Her too. She was what Ma Lou called a specialty item."

"Is that how you ended up on Sycamore?"

"One of the reasons, I suppose. That, and the drugs. When I left that house it was the only thing I knew."

Mother and son sat in their own separate silences. Damian sucked down the last of his coffee and swirled his empty cup in the air, digesting his sordid family history. Janice played with the bracelet on her arm, rolling the one year sobriety charm between her thumb and forefinger as she prayed for strength and guidance.

A random thought made Damian sit up in his chair and plunk his cup on the table. The sound of the empty paper cup reverberating off the wooden table broke through Janice's trance. She looked at Damian wide-eyed and waited for him to reveal what had him roused.

"Was Uncle Earl my daddy? Is that why Aunt Cara kept me?"

Janice gawked at Damian with the confused look of a bird in a cage, trying to figure out why it was entrapped and you were not. She canted her head from side to side, hearing his words but unable to process them. When her mind caught up with her ears Janice let out a loud whoop.

"Hell no!" Janice exclaimed through her laughter.

Her laugh was infectious and Damian couldn't help chuckling, even though he didn't understand why his question was so funny.

"Ooh, you tickle me. I needed that." Janice wiped moisture from her eyes.

"How do you know for sure?"

Janice sobered. "There's one thing I know, lit or not, and that's my own body. Ma Lou made sure of that."

At once, Damian was sorry he'd asked. Every time they seemed to be making progress he opened his mouth and inserted his foot. Seeing the disappointment on his face Janice dismissed the notion with a toss of her hand.

"None of anything that happened is your fault Damian."

"My head knows that, but my heart aches over my selfishness. I never considered anyone else but me."

"You were a child. Who else were you supposed to consider? Listen to me. I know the damage guilt and shame can cause in your life. We should've told you the truth. That was our sin, not yours."

"The truth?"

"The day Aunt Cara found me in the back of Earl's Cadillac; I was already pregnant with you. That fool Earl is not your daddy. Of the three of us I don't know who was more shocked to see who."

"I still don't understand how Aunt Cara ended up where you and Uncle Earl were?"

"Cara had a feeling Earl was cutting out on her, so she'd started following him. He'd gotten lucky up until then."

"She had no idea it was you in the car?"

"That's what she said. Who was I to argue? When Earl rolled down the window I couldn't speak. We just stared at each other. I was expecting to have to fight. I had my knife out ready to cut the woman crazy enough to jump in the backseat after her sorry man. A ho is always at a disadvantage. It helps to keep something sharp on you to even the odds."

"Somehow, I don't think I'll ever make use of your advice, but thanks all the same."

Janice rolled her eyes at Damian. "You never know what you might need."

"I doubt it'll be that. Continue."

"Anyway, Cara and I stayed like that for what felt like forever. Still as statues, mouths open, neither one of us believing what the other was seeing."

Enthralled with her tale, Damian couldn't help showing his impatience when she paused.

"And then?"

"She called my name real soft like. I could barely hear her. She got louder and louder until she was screaming my name. She reached inside the window, unlocked the door and started pounding on Earl. All the while she was screaming my name, she kept screaming my name. Eventually, she flung Earl from the car and climbed in the backseat with me. I didn't know what to do, you know? I couldn't cut her, she was my sister. But I didn't know what she was getting in the car to do. If push came to shove I could take a beating. A ho's got to-"

"Janice, filter, please? Come on."

"Okay sorry. Where was I?"

"Aunt Cara? In the backseat?"

"Oh, yeah. Cara's still screaming, at the top of her lungs now, no tears, just screaming. All of a sudden she grabs me and holds me real tight to her. She starts rocking back and forth squeezing me until I can barely breathe." Janice closed her eyes and wrapped her hands around her elbows, rocking to an invisible beat, lost in her reverie.

Damian waited.

"It felt so good to be...held." Gradually, Janice opened her eyes. She unwrapped her arms from her torso and glanced around the small establishment, embarrassed that her momentary flashback had left her feeling vulnerable.

"But I was stuck, I couldn't move. I remember feeling like if I hugged her back she'd stop. Her mouth was in my ear and I could hear a little whimper coming from her lips. Like a newborn that can't make up its mind if it's sleepy, hungry or just wants you to pick him up. She went on like that for a while and then the sound changed. It became this deep moan. I could feel her stomach vibrating against me. I don't know how to describe it but...her vibrations... they moved through me. No, that's not it."

Janice clenched her fists in frustration. She wanted so badly for Damian to understand what happened in the back of that car. If she could find the right words he'd finally get it.

"They didn't move through me. They were in me. I know it sounds crazy, but at one point I turned my head to look at Cara and she wasn't making a peep. Her eyes were closed and her cheek was resting on my shoulder. It was in me. The sound, the movement, everything, I felt it pushing up in me. I kept swallowing trying to make it go down."

Janice brought her hands to her throat, massaging it. She could feel the weight of it in her windpipe again.

"I swallowed and swallowed but it wouldn't budge. I felt tiny claws scampering over my vocal cords. A voice in my head said 'let it out'. I opened my mouth and what came out was almost...primal. You know?"

Damian could only nod at her description. He'd had many experiences of crying out to God in the early hours of the morning. Sounds he'd never fathomed rumbling in his gut before they forced their way out.

"I broke. I could feel myself crumble, but I was whole. I don't know how long I wailed, but when it was over Cara was right there, holding me still. She rubbed my belly like she knew you were there."

Janice splayed her hands over her now empty womb. Thoughts of Damian swimming inside her made her smile.

"And then?"

"And then she took me home."

"What happened to Uncle Earl?"

"I don't know. He used to drop cash and stuff by the house. Cara never let him in, at least not while I was there. You would know better than me. They get back together?"

"No." Damian snorted.

"What's funny?"

"Growing up, Aunt Cara and I had a little joke between the two of us. I used to call Uncle Earl step-daddy 'cause he never came up farther than the front porch."

"Y'all crazy."

"Okay, so after Aunt Cara took you home, what happened?"

"Life. I was clean up until you were about, two years-old?"

"You're asking me?"

Janice ignored Damian's sarcasm. "Yeah, you were about two. Cara was in the kitchen cooking dinner and you were playing with your blocks in the middle of the floor. All of a sudden I got overwhelmed. I looked at you and all that we had, with Cara, and I felt unworthy, un-clean, unprepared. So, I got up and I left."

"Just like that?"

"Exactly like that. I was gone for about a week. When I came back high, filthy and talking out of my head Cara told me I couldn't stay. I wasn't welcome anymore."

"What about me?"

"I tried to take you with me. Marched right in her house and snatched you out of your highchair. Cara put a whooping on me, and rightly so. That's how you got that scar." Janice reached up and traced the wound that had almost cost Damian his eyesight.

"I saw all that blood and I ran. I did a year and a half in county for injury to a child. I called Cara as soon as I got out. I wanted to make amends, but she told me that you were doing fine without me. She said that if I came back into your life now, it would mess you up. It was an easy lie to believe. You probably would've ended up back with her anyway. I was a mess."

"We'll never know, will we? I can't believe she lied to me."

"You can't be mad at her. Honestly, she probably did the best thing for you. I mean look at you now." Janice proclaimed, opening her arms wide as if she were putting Damian on display.

Uncomfortable with her assessment Damian looked at his watch feigning interest in the time. If he left now he could get away without the conversation turning to him.

"You have somewhere to be?"

"Yes," he lied with ease, even changing his voice to a formal tone so she wouldn't question the validity of his answer. "I have a few counseling sessions lined up this evening. I need to pray and connect with God to get in the right mind set."

Damian barely flinched when he invoked God's name into his deception. As they stood to leave, Janice leaned in for a hug. Damian automatically took a step back from her advance before he could control his reflexes. Her pride was injured, but she recovered quickly.

"Too soon?" she asked off-handedly.

"A little."

"Do you think we could meet again?" Before Damian could answer, Janice dug in her purse for a pen and paper to write down her number.

Hastily she wrote her number down with a ball-point Bic on an old receipt. She shoved the wrinkled paper at Damian. He didn't have the heart to not reach out for it.

"I'll call you," he lied again, a skill that was becoming too easy for him. Damian shoved the number in his suit pocket and left the café without a backward glance.

| 13 |

Bishop Thomas sat at the head of a long wooden table. Ten couples sat around him enraptured by his motivating speech.

"As you can see it's up to us to fill in the gap that's been left by Pastor Fellows. The people of God should not perish because they lack leadership. And as my Granny used to say; one monkey don't stop no show." He said showing his country charm. Playing up the schtick made people feel at ease. Made them feel like they were smarter than the country bumpkin in front of them.

That was the trick. Hit them with enough syllables to show you were educated, let them know you knew how to handle business. Mix that with enough chagrin to appear humble and keep them feeling superior and you had a recipe for a successful long con.

"That's good, that's good." Bro. Dominic Trippler agreed.

"There are people in this world who need our help. People without the basic necessities of life. No education, no running water, no food and no clothes. Imagine standing before your maker having had the opportunity and choosing not to help the least of these?"

Appeal to their sense of charity. Their need to assuage themselves of the guilt their money has bought them.

"What God is asking is not much. Ten thousand dollars per family is all that's required to be a blessing and a life changer to someone who doesn't have a tenth of what you have."

They didn't quite buy it yet. He could tell from the expression on their faces. Rich people were a finicky bunch and rich church folks were both finicky and cheap. For five years he'd bided his time sucking up to these nouveau riche debutants. *They will not ruin this for me.*

"Let's look at the big picture here folks. I don't mean any harm, but let's put all of our cards on the table. I think I speak for not only myself but for everyone one here when I say that if you don't have the money we will all understand."

"None of us are hurting for money," Bro. Sean Cleaver quipped, "it's just that with the economy the way it is we can't afford to be throwing money around haphazardly."

"And I wouldn't want you to. I'm not trying to rush anyone here." *Stop giving me shit.* "I understand if you don't want to invest right now, but I have a confession to make. Living Waters was not supposed to be a part of this deal."

"What do you mean?" Sis. Carmen Cleaver asked.

"I mean the charity we're supplementing did not want Living Waters involved in this project." *Vanity kills. I hope they choke on it.*

Murmurs echoed through the room.

"They said we weren't ready to handle a commitment of this magnitude. They thought a mega church like Hail Emmanuel was better suited to handle their needs. I told them that they were mistaken. After all, we may not be as sophisticated, worldly or successful as the place up the street but when I look around the room I'm reminded of our brother Moses. Abandoned at birth, driven away from the place he grew up and a speech impediment to boot. All of those strikes against him and God still called him to do a great work in His name."

"He was a mighty man," declared Sis. Chandra Jacobs

"Yes he was," agreed Bishop Thomas. "And as mighty as he was when our Lord God came to him and told him He was going to use him as an instrument, Moses wasn't ready. In His wisdom and sovereignty God saw his potential and He pushed him forward. Now I'm not God and Lord knows I don't want to be pushy, but I do believe that God is calling you all to a higher purpose, to serve Him and help His people."

"I have a question." Sis. Rayelle Morgan raised one hand while the other played with the Mikimoto Black South Sea pearl necklace her husband's new money bought.

"Yes Sis. Morgan?"

"Rayelle, please."

"Ok Sis. Rayelle. What can I do you for?" Thomas showed the smallest amount of teeth behind the thinnest smile he could muster through his frustration. They were ripe for his plucking. Every time he got them to the point where they were eating out of his hands, she asked a question and he had to start priming the pump all over again.

"Well, umm forgive me for interrupting."

"It's alright. I want y'all to feel secure in your transactions. Ask all the questions you like." *Stupid bitch. Sitting there twirling those damn pearls, trying to appear dignified. Who in the hell wears black pearls anyway? Don't even look real.*

"Well, I mean I'm all for helping the less fortunate," her twirling increased with each syllable, "but isn't ten-thousand dollars quite a bit of startup money? That's one-hundred thousand dollars total. Couldn't we build them a new country for all that?"

Nervous laughter cascaded up and down the table. Bishop Thomas's ripe fruit was starting to rot on the vine. Heads that once nodded in agreement with his grand plan now bobbed their dissent.

Ten thousand dollars was chump change to these people. Everyone sitting around this table knew it. They were his chosen ones. He'd researched them all, worked on them for several months. Hints dropped here and there to test them out. When Pastor Fellows took a mysterious leave of absence a doorway was opened and Bishop Thomas boldly walked through.

It was the opportunity of a lifetime, a chance for him to pull off the con of the century. All he needed to make his master plan complete was a fall guy. The thought nagged at him but the timing was too perfect.

Thomas chuckled like an over indulgent nephew pacifying his delu-
sional auntie. "Do you know what it cost to keep up a tiny village, let
alone run a whole country?" *Now answer that with your good talking ass.*

"I can't say that I know the exact amount." Mrs. Morgan answered.
Embarrassed, she looked around the room searching for backup. Finding only hung heads she faltered in her confidence and gave Thomas
the ammunition he needed.

Thomas let his gaze fall on every individual before coming back to
rest solely on Rayelle. Everything was riding on this moment. The first
dog to yelp is the one who hurts the most. All he needed was one yelp.

"Of course WE have the money." Marion O'Neal interjected. His
wife Jackie held his hand in solidarity not wanting anyone to believe
that they were too cheap to put up their portion of the money.

Yelp.

"What about y'all?" He asked Bro. and Sis. Friendly pointedly.

"Yes!" They answered in unison.

I gotta bring it home. Thomas contorted his face and furrowed his
brow, purposely allowing his theatrics to lengthen the uncomfortable
silence. Bringing his hands together dramatically with a loud thunder-
ous clap, he was finally ready to move forward.

"Can I ask you a question saints?" He didn't wait for a proper response from the group. Instead he kept going, posing theological questions in a rapid fire succession in hopes of keeping them off balanced.
"How much do you suppose it costs to get into the kingdom of heaven?
Doesn't the bible say that faith without works is dead? Are we supposed
to shore up our treasures in heaven or on earth?"

Once again he perused the faces of every member of the group,
judging their righteousness with his eyes. The scratching sound of pen
on paper as Bro. Friendly hurriedly wrote out a check for ten thousand
dollars was like the sound of a perfectly tuned Stradivari to Thomas's
ears. When Bro.'s Morgan, Jordan, Trippler and Sis. Cleaver followed
suit, it turned the room into a quartet.

Yelp. Yelp.

Determined not to be outdone by the others Bro.'s O'Neal, Boston, Simpson, Maxwell and Sis. Jacobs formed their own orchestra. The crescendo coming with the uniformed ripping of perforated pads.

Yelp. Yelp. Yelp.

| 14 |

"Hello Lakefield, Tracy Phillips here from WJKZ Channel 6 News, your prime source for what's happening in your neighborhood. I'm coming to you live with an update on the Living Waters Circle Scam. When we spoke earlier police were still looking for Bishop Anthony Thomas and Junior Pastor Damian Hardwin.

We've just been informed by the FBI that they've traced most of the money and are close to seizing all of the stolen funds. The trail begins with a personal account of Bishop Thomas at a local Lakefield Barnett Bank. The funds were then transferred to an account under the Living Waters umbrella with Damian Hardwin as the primary holder.

Here's where things get interesting folks. The funds were then split into two separate accounts with Hardwin as the primary. One account was opened out of the west coast based TriStar National Bank while the other account was opened out of the Canadian based Republic Bank and Trust. It seems that these two funds were set up to automatically siphon one dollar every day from not only the members of the Circle Scam but also 30 other accounts from members of other churches up and down the Eastern Seaboard.

From there another account was discovered, also opened under Hardwin's name in the Cayman Islands, through Propriety International Bank. This account had money dumped into it monthly from the TriStar and Republic bank accounts. Through their investigation bank officials say funds typically stayed in this account for less than one hour before they were bounced to another overseas account in the Philippines. Authorities are currently trying to gain access to that account. According to officials the money trail may not end there.

You heard it here first. The Circle Scam has gone international. A source at Interpol, who has agreed to speak with us off the record due to the highly classified nature of this case, tells us that money laundering schemes like this one are becoming more frequent and elaborate due to the internet and the lax laws that regulate them. According to our anonymous source one of the difficulties in prosecuting these embezzlement cases is tracking down who actually opened the accounts because all the necessary documents are signed electronically.

Right now it looks like Bishop Thomas is the front man and Pastor Hardwin is the mastermind behind the Circle Scam at Living Waters. We want to know what you think Lakefield. Go to www.wjkzinvestigate.net and tell us who you think is behind the fleecing of the flock. Is it the elderly convict who's spent his last days preaching the gospel or is it the young, hungry minister trying to make a name for himself? You choose.

In the meantime keep your televisions tuned to WJKZ, Channel 6 News, you're prime source for what's happening in your neighborhood. We now return you to your regularly scheduled programming."

| 15 |

Pastor Fellows trusted him to watch over Living Waters and he'd failed. When Damian replayed it in his mind it was so easy to see Bishop Thomas's lies. So much was going on. Mother Wilson was always yammering in his ear about her son being appointed to the Board. Bishop Thomas was everywhere and in everything keeping members riled up about lost sheep with no shepherd. Shonen was constantly telling him to look out for Bishop Thomas.

Women were throwing themselves at him. Members were leaving the church. New people that he never got a chance to meet or get to know were streaming in. The entire culture of the church was changing right before his eyes and there was nothing he could do about it.

Living Waters was supposed to be a family. Pastor Fellows made an impression on him his junior year of seminary school. He was a regular guest speaker and part time Professor at Southern Georgia Seminary School. Unlike some of the other ministers who seemed to be more interested in scouting out their competition than mentoring, Pastor Fellows actually took time out to speak with new pastors personally.

On the day he gave his senior presentation Fellows surprised him by being front and center. Afterwards he took him out to dinner and asked him to sit under him at Living Waters. Damian was honored at the request and immediately felt a quickening in his spirit that this was the place he was supposed to be.

The two were inseparable. Fellows was more than a superior, he was the father Damian never had. He'd bonded with Tristine and Cameron, Fellows wife and daughter, as well. Over the years Fellows counseled him, helped him maneuver through the pitfalls of new ministers and opened his home to him. He'd introduced him to Shonen and other solid men in the church and Damian gained a few uncles in the process. Fellows, Shonen and others like them helped usher him into spiritual manhood.

When he received a late afternoon phone call from Fellows that Tristine had emptied everything out of the house and taken Cameron he was heartbroken not only for his mentor, but for himself. He felt as if they'd abandoned him also. There was a kinship and solidarity in their mutual hurt and betrayal. A feeling he was all too familiar with.

Fellows made it clear that he was the only one who knew. Not even Shonen was aware of what was going on. Damian vowed to keep his secret, even though he knew it was wrong. How could he judge his father, his friend for wanting time to heal away from the prying eyes and loose tongues of people like Mother Wilson?

Out of a desperate need to protect and support a man who'd given him a home and a place to belong Damian had gone along with Fellows suggestion that he fill-in for him. Initially, it was a meeting here or there, then bible study, leadership conferences and then he had him sitting with the Elder Board on a permanent basis. The congregation was used to Damian preaching first and fifth Sundays. So seeing him in the pulpit on second, third and fourth Sundays weren't hard for them to get used to.

Too much had been heaped on Damian's capable yet inexperienced and naïve shoulders. He began to resent his newfound responsibilities. With Fellows removing himself almost entirely from everything he felt like he'd been tricked. Things were getting out of hand. Damian felt trapped in a prison cell of his own making, Fellows' secret the only key to free him. He thought he was doing a good thing when Bishop Thomas approached him about spearheading a charity he'd kick started.

* * *

Bishop Thomas startled Damian as he was rounding the corner in the hallway of Living Waters' administrative offices. There'd been some talk going around the rumor mill about secret meetings between Bishop Thomas and some of the more affluent members of the congregation. Great, Damian thought to himself, one more thing to take care of.

"Hey, Thomas. Just the man I was looking for."

"Watch out there young man. What can I do you for?"

"Let's talk down in my office." Damian offered.

"Sure youngster."

Thomas was getting under Damian's skin with all the undercover inference to his age and inexperience. They reached Damian's office with a soft sheen of tension glimmering between them.

"Come in," Damian opened the door and gestured with his hand, "take a seat."

"Mighty kind of you."

Damian took a seat behind his desk, cleared his throat and decided to suspense with the niceties and get to business. "Well, let's get to it."

"Let's!" Bishop Thomas proclaimed with too much enthusiasm.

"There's been some discussion about meetings that you've been having with the Tripplers, O'Neals, Greens and Morgans."

Damian waited, not wanting to give Thomas any clues as to how much he actually knew. It was Shonen who'd come to him with the news of the secret meetings. He cautioned him to be careful, but Shonen was always cautioning him. It didn't make sense to him. If Fellows could trust him, then why couldn't he catch a break with Shonen?

"Yes?"

Damian was not in the mood to play with the old man. "Who sanctioned the meetings?"

Now we're getting somewhere, thought Thomas. From Damian's question he knew that he didn't know anything. He was fishing. There was money involved, lots of money. No one asks who got their permission slip signed when there's money involved. Thomas reminded himself that he was still in need of a fall guy.

"Look son, the truth is, well maybe I should start from the beginning."

"Go ahead," Damian encouraged, "start wherever you'd like."

"Can I be candid with you for a minute?"

"Sure." Slightly annoyed, Damian only wanted to get this inquiry over with so he could study for Sunday's sermon.

"I don't mean to insult anyone here Damian. I mean I understand the difficult task that you've been given. And I'm not at all suggesting that anything is necessarily your fault."

"What are you talking about? What does any of this have to do with the meetings?"

Thomas looked dismayed. "I'm sorry. I was sure you'd noticed."

This is getting old. "Noticed what?"

"Noticed...the condition of things. How the atmosphere around here," Thomas twirled his fingers in a circular motion around his head, "has changed."

Thomas saw a light ignite in Damian's eyes. Patience, young buck. His comment about change struck a chord. Not sure which ace he was holding would get him the desired result Thomas decided to drop the other one later to seal the deal.

"Go on."

"When I came to Living Waters there seemed to be more of a community feel to the church. How do you young people say it? There was a different 'vibe'. People cared for each other more, did more for each other."

Thomas wasn't a fool. He knew he couldn't out preach, out teach or out seminary Damian. What he could do and would do with a raw talent marveling Sebastian Bach's, was play beautiful music with his heart strings. The research he'd done on all of them when he came to Living Waters would be vital to his big score. Damian's background had been a little convoluted but once he found out that his mother had been from the same hometown as him finding out what made him tick wasn't hard to come by.

He vaguely remembered Janice, but he was very familiar with the rest of the family, especially Ruth Ann. There was a time when the White folk's graveyard was the hot spot for young boys in Topaux,

Mississippi. The things that girl would let them do to her for next to nothing. It was shameful. With a family history like that the boy was easy enough to read and manipulate.

"There have been a few changes. We've grown a lot. Sometimes it's hard to keep that intimacy," he reasoned.

"Sometimes. Other times it's a lack of good leadership."

Damian started to speak, but Thomas interrupted his rebuttal. It was time to play his other ace.

"Like I said before, I'm not making any judgment calls about you or laying any blame at your feet. What I'm simply saying is that Mario left some big shoes to fill. I think we can both agree that with the way things went down it left a bad taste in some people's mouth."

"How so?"

"Come on, Damian. I know people trust you and I know you don't want to violate that trust, but it's just us." Getting comfortable, Thomas leaned back in his chair. His demeanor said that this was a casual talk between friends.

By comparison Damian's body language was tense. Sitting on the edge of his seat, his emotions were getting the better of him.

"You really don't know?"

"No, no one's said anything to me."

"I can't believe this. Wow." Thomas stood up, hands on his hips and gave Damian the most solemn look of despair. "No one has spoken to you about the situation with Tristine?"

Now it was Damian's turn to look distressed. "You know?"

When you're alone in a 3 x 5 room with its own built in bathroom, you have a lot of time to master facial expressions. Incredulous was a good one to have in your cache.

"Doesn't everyone?"

The balloon Damian had been carrying in his chest for the past 6 months had finally been punctured. Relief washed over him.

Got him.

| 16 |

Maveth turned up his nose at the lies Bishop Thomas spewed. The putridness of rotting flesh overwhelmed him.

"Racham, how can this one still claim to be human?"

"Have death and sin not been his constant companions? His soul has decayed beyond repair." Racham shrugged off Maveth's concerns.

"Is he of no consequence to us now?"

"Only so much as his place in the life of the one we were sent for."

"What now, brother?"

"Have you received a word that is contrary to the Master's?"

Exasperated and light headed from the stench, "No, Racham. You know very well that I have not," Maveth replied.

Racham waited for his companion to answer the question he put forth.

"What is time, when He holds the world inside of his hand? Of course, we wait."

"Yes, Maveth, we wait. Be of good cheer," Racham teased his friend, "our waiting will not be in vain."

| 17 |

Damian sat back for a minute and thought. If everyone knew then there was no secret to keep. This was a good thing. But why hadn't Fellows told him? Why was he hearing this from Thomas? And what did this have to do with the meetings?

"That's a relief, but what does that have to do with the meetings? Are you planning something for his return?"

"In a manner of speaking."

Thomas made sure he had Damian's full attention before he continued. He locked eyes with him and held Damian there until he was ready to speak.

"I've always been upfront about my past Damian."

Damian swallowed involuntarily. Thomas watched as his Adams apple bobbed up and down, the non-verbal tell brandishing Damian a liar.

"Even though I've made peace with the mistakes in my past, I understand that other people, even good Christian people, might not be so forgiving."

"Perception can be hard to overcome."

"It's funny ain't it? As much grace as God extends us on the daily basis and some people are too holy to give an old man another chance. Oh well," Thomas conceded, "such is life."

"Such is life," Damian agreed.

"Oh well, like I was saying, I've been missing the community aspect of Living Waters. So, I did some homework, got a few like-minded people together and started a charity to help disadvantaged children in Honduras."

"You started a charity?"

"To be clear, we didn't start the charity. The charity was already in place. We started a charity circle here at Living Waters."

Damian couldn't believe what he was hearing. Had he been that out of touch with what was going on right under his nose?

"Under whose authority?"

"Hear me out first, please? I know what you're thinking and I don't blame you. Give me the opportunity to explain."

Thomas leaned forward in the chair bending at the waist. Clasping his hands together and letting his head hang, he purposely mimicked a posture of supplication to Damian's superior position.

"I'm listening, but this needs to start making sense soon." Damian drummed his fingers lightly on his desk, his frustration growing and his patience thinning.

"Okay, that's fair," Thomas said sitting up. He paused, pretending to get his thoughts together, keeping his hands firmly clasped together as if pleading for forgiveness. His voice came out in a hushed tone with a slight tremor. "I saw a void Pastor. It seemed to me that Living Waters was losing its way. I wanted to do something to get us back on track."

"Why the secrecy?"

"I'm an old man with a record. I turned my life around and I've made a decent living traveling around spreading the gospel. In all that, what I never had was a real home. I've never known people I could depend on and who could depend on me."

Like an expert manipulator Thomas let a single tear drop from his watery eyes before wiping it away with the flat of his palm. Damian pushed the box of tissues he kept on his desk for emotional counseling sessions at him. Thomas waved them away and made a show of composing himself.

"I admit as a man that my pride got the best of me. I wanted to prove that I was a valuable asset around here, that I could do something and make a difference."

"I admire your efforts and I even sympathize with your issues of self-worth. Surely, you have to understand that we can't have secret groups meeting without any headship?"

"I do. I thought if I could establish something, sort of have everything together then people could see that I wasn't just an old convict to be put out to pasture. I figured when it was successful it would be a nice welcome home present for Pastor Fellows."

Damian checked his watch. Thomas could tell the young minister was losing his patience. It was now or never. If he didn't take advantage of Damian's impatience he might never get another chance for his big payoff.

"None of that matters now anyway. I guess it was the foolish hopes of an old man to think we could make a difference. It's a shame too. We've done a lot to help those kids. Because of our little group those children have had a steady supply of food, water and some of them have been able to go to school for the first time."

"We were this close," Thomas pinched his thumb and forefinger together showing a quarter inch of space between them, "to building a school for them."

"Tell you what, send me the information for the charity and I'll look it over."

Damian stood up signaling a close to the meeting.

"Thank-you so much Pastor Hardwin." Thomas followed Damian's lead. He extended his hand so they could shake, but didn't immediately let go. "There's one more thing I hate to trouble you with."

"What's that?" Damian relaxed the muscles in his fingers so he could disengage from the handshake Thomas wouldn't release. The old man didn't seem to take the hint, leaving Damian's hand trapped in Thomas's vice grip.

Thomas spoke fast, hoping Damian's need to be free of him was greater than his attention to detail. "I've been using my own personal account to transfer money to the charity. Unfortunately, we collected a little over 10,000.00 and the IRS is breathing down my neck and because of my past they're trying to freeze the money to the kids because it's on foreign soil and they're set to get their school uniforms this week and-"

"What do you need from me?"

"Since, everything's out in the open now we could come underneath your headship. If you open up an account for us, through Living Waters, the children can go to school and-"

"I don't know about that. I'm really busy now. Until Fellows comes back my plate is overflowing."

Thomas finally released Damian's hand and went back to a pleading stance. He slouched down in a small bow, maneuvering himself in front of the door and continuing to petition his case.

"I understand, but if you think about it everything is already set up. I've done the research; we already have a reliable, reputable charity and real people that we're helping. There's really nothing for you to do except open the account."

"Get me the data and I'll think about it. That's the best I can do."

Thomas moved from the door conceding his defeat.

"I'll get you the data but this is about the kids. If we don't move the money now they'll never have a chance. I don't want them to have to pay for my mistakes. They're like the children I never had. They deserve the opportunity to be better than the circumstances they were born into."

"You swear this is a legitimate charity?"

"I put it on everything I know and love."

"If, and I mean if, I decide to do this you can't burn me on this. I'm putting my complete trust in you."

"It's a skinny ledge you'd be stepping out on and I appreciate that. I won't let you down."

"Ok, ok. It's too late to go now. Meet me at First Georgia Bank off Main and Jackson first thing in the morning."

"Praise Him!" Thomas exclaimed. "Praise His Holy name!"

Thomas put his arms around Damian and wrapped him up in an enormous bear hug. Real tears were running down his face as he thumped Damian on the back.

"Alright. Alright," Damian said grabbing Thomas by the shoulders, putting some distance between him and the older man.

"Thank you Pastor, thank you," Thomas said, backing up to the door. He felt for the knob behind him and was leaving the office when Damian called out to him.

"Bishop Thomas, don't forget to get me that info."

| 18 |

Damian pulled into the parking lot of First Georgia Bank at 9:05 to see Thomas sitting on a bench outside the bank. The lot was already filled with early rising patrons, forcing Damian to swing into the first available spot he could find. Flipping down the sun visor, he grabbed his glasses, placing the dark tinted lens over his eyes before he exited the vehicle.

It was almost like there was a cloud shadowing him from the time he put his feet on the floor. He tried praying in the shower, but he lost track in the middle and started going over his to do list instead. By the time he got to the bank he'd convinced himself that the only thing he was suffering from was a much needed vacation that he promised himself he would take the minute Pastor Fellows hit the church doors.

The two men greeted each other with a handshake and a side hug outside of the bank.

"Hey Pastor Hardwin, glad you made it."

"Thomas. Let's get this done. Did you bring the data on the charity?"

"Oh, no sorry, I didn't know what your schedule was like this morning. I dropped by the church and put the file under your door before I came."

"That's cool, let's get inside."

Damian opened the door letting Thomas step into the bank first. Thomas' pulse sped up to pounding when he entered the bank. If anyone cared to pay close enough attention they would see his carotid artery dancing in his neck.

"Hello gentlemen, welcome to First Georgia Bank. My name is Callie Marshall" announced the cheery blond southern belle greeting them in the lobby, "how may we service you today?"

"Hi Ms. Marshall," Damian responded, "my name is Damian Hardwin from Living Waters and this is my associate Bishop Anthony Thomas. We need to open a new commercial account today."

"Well you've definitely come to the right place gentlemen and call me Callie. We're all family around here. Do you mind if I call you by your first names?"

"Sure," they answered in unison.

"You can call me Thomas, everybody else does," Anthony added.

"Thank you, I appreciate it Damian , Thomas. Follow me. We'll go to my office and discuss the details."

Callie walked to her glass enclosed office, Damian and Thomas in tow.

"Have a seat gentlemen. Can I get either of you a water, soda or sweet tea?" she asked, planting herself in her high back leather chair.

"I'll have a sweet tea, darling."

"What about you Damian? Can I get you anything?"

"I'm good, thanks. On second thought I'll take a water."

"Coming right up." Callie pressed the intercom button on her phone and spoke into the microphone. "Darien?"

"Yes, Ms. Marshall?"

"Darien be a dear and get me two waters and a sweet tea please?"

"On my way, Ms. Marshall."

"My assistant, he's an absolute peach." Callie explained in a low conspiratorial tone as she hung up the phone. "Tell you what, while we're waiting for Darien we'll take care of a few formalities and get you started."

Callie was reaching into her desk for the new account forms when a spectacled, middle aged man wearing dark slacks, a long sleeved lemon colored button up and a multi colored plaid bow-tie knocked on the doorframe of her office.

"Oh, that was fast. Damian, Thomas this is my assistant Darien Swissman. He's another valuable member of our First Georgia team."

"Hi!" Darien the assistant waved emphatically with one hand and with practiced skill balanced a tray of drinks in the other.

Both men nodded their heads in acknowledgement.

"Here you go sirs," Darien said, putting a glass of water on a coaster in front of Damian and a glass of tea on an identical coaster for Thomas. "And for you madam," he said bowing playfully and putting Callie's drink directly in her hand. Darien set the half empty bottle of Evian Sparkling Water and the pitcher of sweet tea on a small end table in between Callie's desk and the book shelf closest to Thomas

"Anything else I can do for you Ms. Marshall?"

"No, I think that will be all."

"Call me if you need me," Darien the assistant called over his shoulder as he darted out of the office.

"Alright, down to business, here you go Damian." Callie said handing Damian a stack of forms in triplicate to complete. "You can use my desk to fill these out. Will you be an authorized user on the account Anthony?"

"No." Damian and Thomas answered at the same time.

Thomas cleared his throat, not quite liking the tone Damian used when he replied to Callie's inquiry. "I won't be an authorized user, but I do need to transfer funds from our charity into the new account."

"Ok, we can definitely take care of that for you." Callie rotated her chair so she could sign in to her computer. She tapped on the keyboard with quick efficient strokes while Damian scooted his chair forward to fill out the papers Callie gave him.

"Let me ask you a few questions while you're doing that. What was the name of the organization you're affiliated with again?"

Damian looked up at Callie briefly before answering, "Living Waters Congregation. We already have a corporate account with you."

"I knew that name sounded familiar." Callie typed in Living Waters and watched as the details of the account scrolled up on the screen. "You did say the principal use for the account is for a charity?"

"Yes." This time Thomas piped up for Damian.

"Then we don't want to use the main account, but we can make it come under the umbrella of Living Waters Congregation. Since you're already an authorized user on that account Damian I have all the information I need to start the charity account. I will need to see your Georgia Driver's License to verify your identity."

Damian reached in his back pocket and fished out his license from his wallet. He placed the laminated card on the desk and pushed it towards Callie. She picked it up, tilting it in the light to raise the 3D Georgia state seal on the card and read over the information. Her eyes shifted to her computer as she compared the information in her hand with the information on the screen.

"Looks like you check out. Here you go." Callie slid the license back to Damian and he quickly placed it back in his wallet.

Damn, missed it! Thomas chastised himself. You are gonna blow it if you don't get it together. He didn't expect for Damian to pick his license up so fast. He thought he'd be too preoccupied with the paperwork and leave it on the desk.

"Thomas? Thomas?"

"Huh?" Thomas was jostled out of his thoughts. Callie and Damian shared identical looks of worry when he finally became aware of his surroundings.

"Are you ok?"

Thomas laughed off Callie's concern. "The Lord willing and the creek don't rise. Y'all don't worry about me darling. I was just thinking about how God can take a man's sorry life and use it for His good."

"Amen," Damian cosigned before going back to his paperwork.

"Amen," Callie chimed in. "He sure can."

"What'd I miss, Ms. Callie, while I was on my trip down memory lane?"

"I was asking you about your charity's name."

"That's easy enough, it's Cazador de Sueños. It means dreamcatcher in Spanish. We help poor kids get food, clothes, and school supplies. Did you know that in Honduras they won't let you go to school if you don't have a uniform? Who can think about what they're wearing when you can't eat?"

"Oh my goodness, those poor children, I couldn't even imagine. I like what you're doing for them. That's real nice. Now how do you spell that?"

Thomas beamed for Callie and took his time spelling out Cazador de Suenos keeping one eye trained on Damian's progress.

"You have the account information for the transfer?"

"Yeah, I have it right here in my wallet." Thomas retrieved his wallet from the inside of his sports coat pocket and took his time leafing through the cards in his billfold. He passed over the card with his personal account number written in neat block letters three times before he saw Damian's hand drop down to the signature line on the last form.

Thomas timed it so that he was handing Callie his card half a second before Damian was putting the finishing touch on the banking contract. Reading upside down was a mandatory survival skill in prison. Thomas leaned forward, refilling his cup from the pitcher, putting himself at an angle to scan every piece of paper on Callie's desk. When Damian turned the documents upside down so Callie could read them, Thomas committed his social security number and the church's tax free identification number to memory.

Callie wrote down the new account number on a card identical to Thomas's with First Georgia Bank and its logo embossed on the top. Instead of handing it directly to Damian she put it on top of Thomas's worn card. He sucked down what was left in his glass and then leaned over again to refill from the pitcher. He discreetly stored the new account number in his head and set back. Damian looked at him out of the corner of his eye, but didn't say anything.

"Thirsty," Thomas offered as an explanation and loosened his tie to bring home the point.

"That's it. We're all finished." Callie stood, handed Damian the new account card and shook their hands.

"It was a pleasure doing business with y'all. Let me walk you to the door."

Damian stopped Callie with an upheld hand. "Don't trouble yourself Callie. Thanks for your help, we can see our way out."

"Okay then. Don't hesitate to call me if you need anything."

As they walked out of Callie's office Darien looked up from his typing and gave another spastic wave to Damian and Thomas. "Have a good day gentlemen."

"You too," they replied.

Their business concluded Damian and Thomas said their goodbyes and started to go their separate ways. Thomas waited a few beats and then shouted Damian's name across the parking lot. He ran over to Damian pretending to be out of breath from the exertion. He even added a slight limp for good measure.

"Glad I caught you," he wheezed.

"What's up?"

"What do you want to do about future deposits? I can't always get across town to make a face to face deposit. You know I bank at Community Bank on the East side. I don't think it's fair to put the responsibility on anyone else."

"So what do you propose we do?"

"Well," Thomas rolled his eyes upwards like he was seriously contemplating Damian's solicitation instead of stalling for time. His suggestion couldn't look as if it were preplanned. Either way Damian would end up in the driver's seat and Thomas's culpability would be limited. "You could give me the account number and I could continue to make the deposits from my account to the Living Waters account on the computer?"

"I really think we should keep this as official as possible. That means no more deposits from your personal account." This is exactly what I didn't want. "For now, until I can get someone to personally take this over, give me whatever money you collect and I'll deposit it myself."

"That'll work, but most of the members prefer to do electronic transfers directly into my account, you know, for their own security."

Lightning bolts were firing behind Damian's right eye making it spasm. "Fine. Here's the number. I shouldn't have to tell you this but only give it out to those people who are already using the electronic deposit method. No one new. Are we clear?"

"Crystal, Pastor Hardwin."

"I've gotta go, I'm already running behind schedule. I'll see you at the leadership conference?"

"Yes, sir."

| 19 |

"We interrupt your program for a quick update on the previously reported Living Waters Circle Scam. I am joined by religious expert Dr. Tom Preshing. You may know our special guest as the author of the controversial New York Times best seller 'Temple Sheeple: How Religion Herds the Masses'. He'll be giving us his insight into this peculiar situation."

"Hello Tom, it's good to have you here with us."

"Hi Tracy, I'm glad to be here."

"We previously reported that Bishop Anthony Thomas and Pastor Damian Hardwin were on the run and that Senior Pastor Mario Fellows was unavailable for comment. While we regret to inform you that police have yet to apprehend the two alleged con men, we now have an official statement from Pastor Fellows. The Senior Pastor is quoted as saying:

"A great disservice has been done to the body of Christ, its members and to the people of Lakefield. I sincerely apologize for leaving the gate open and allowing this evil into the church. I pray that both believers and nonbelievers alike can find peace and healing in this terrible time of upheaval."

"Wow Tom, gates opening, evil creeping in? That's some pretty scary stuff. What's your take on Pastor Fellow's statement?"

"Well, Tracy, this is classic religious manipulation."

"Religious manipulation? I'm intrigued, how so?"

"Religion has been used as a way to both tame and insight the masses ignorant enough to believe in the ultimate magicians trick for thou-

70 - KALIMAH WILLIAMS

sands of years. I mean think about it, the person who can tap into the religious subconscious successfully has the power to control civilization. Religion, and by rote religious leaders, know this and as we see in the 'Circle Scam' they use it to their personal benefit, at the expense of people who just want to believe in something."

"So, do you doubt the sincerity and validity of Pastor Fellow's statement?"

"Yes, wholeheartedly, and emphatically so. The truth of the matter, Tracy, is there is no God. It's a fabrication, an illusion. What people are seeing now is that religion cannot be trusted. Forget prostitution, religion is the oldest professional con in the world."

"Thank you Tom. Hopefully, you'll stay with us as this story unfolds."

"I'd be delighted."

"We now return you to your regularly scheduled program already in progress.

* * *

Two figures stood in the shadows of the newsroom watching the events unfold.

"Is this one serious?" Maveth inquired already knowing the answer.

"Sadly, it seems so."

"This human has the audacity to speak of the Master in this fashion?"

Racham, seeing Maveth's eyes grow in heat and intensity stays his hand afraid of what might happen next.

"No, Maveth! This one is not our mission. Can you punish him for executing the free will our Master has given him?"

"Perhaps, I can't, but to say these abominations after all He has done?"

"This Tom Preshing's time will come, just like every other creature who has doubted. He has not committed the unforgivable, is there not still hope for him?"

Maveth did not share his counterparts' optimism; it was not in his nature.

"Come," Racham beckoned, *"do we not still have much to do?"*

| 20 |

Pastor Fellows sat with his Bible opened to Psalms 32:3-5:

When I kept silent my bones wasted away through my groaning all day long. For day and night your hand was heavy upon me my strength was sapped as in the heat of summer. Then I acknowledged my sin to you and did not cover up my iniquity. I said I will confess my transgressions to the Lord. And you forgave the guilt of my sin.

"God, how do I come back to you when all of it's my fault?" Stubborn tears ran down his cheeks, into his open mouth. Everything Mario kept bottled up inside him, rushed out. He'd wasted so much time in the dark, hiding, afraid to face his truth.

Mario let his mind wander to better days. Days when his family was intact and his body and spirit were somewhat whole.

They weren't a perfect match, but what they had fit. At least it did to him. Tristine never fully saw the vision of being a pastor's wife, but Mario figured being his wife was a good start. The rest, he thought, would come in time.

* * *

They met at Perkins University in Atlanta, Georgia. Mario was in the last year of his Doctorate of Divinity degree, while Tristine was in the middle of earning her Master's in Political Science. He was on his way to an Approaches to Asian Religion class when he saw her across the quad. Her skin shone like a bar of Hershey's Special Dark Chocolate, her smile captured his heart and her eyes took the rest of him. At that moment she owned him and he didn't even know her name.

His feet headed North and turned East on their own accord. Before he could register what was happening, Mario was standing in front of his mystery woman and her friends, trying to recover from the long silence that followed his impromptu visitation.

"Can we help you?" she teased.

"Um, I was going to class," was all Mario could get out.

She wasn't one of those women who enjoyed seeing a man squirm so she could embarrass him. Instead she took pity on him, hooked her arm in his and led him away from the group. When they were a safe distance away from the crowd, with a minimum amount of privacy she dropped his arm and waited patiently.

"Hi," she finally said when it didn't look like he was going to break the ice.

It was the kick start he needed to come back to his senses.

"Hey," he smiled shyly, "I'm Mario."

"Hey," she said mocking him lightly, "I'm Tristine."

They became inseparable. She pushed him and he challenged her. Both of them working towards the same goals; starting a family, building a life together and flourishing in their careers.

The day Tristine graduated, Mario proposed. Instinctively, she started screaming yes the moment his hand reached into his pocket to take out the small box. Mario motioned for her to hold out her hand so he could test the fit. The half carat princess cut diamond nestled comfortably around the base of her finger.

Tristine looked down lovingly at the ring, her head swimming with thoughts of becoming Mrs. Mario Fellows. She stood up to hug Mario and her knees buckled unexpectedly causing her to fall into his arms.

"Be careful baby," Mario cautioned, holding her up until she became steady on her feet.

"Wow, I don't know what happened."

"Don't worry about it," he reassured, "I got you."

Mario pulled Tristine close to him, wrapping his arms around her tightly, repeating his vow softly in her ear, "I got you, I got you, I got you. I promise."

"I'm okay, just clumsy," she reasoned before hiding her face in his chest. It was a poor excuse for the truth but it was all she could think was, *I'm going to be a preacher's wife.*

* * *

From the beginning she'd told him that she would stand by his side, but that she didn't want to be phony and stand up before the church and represent something she wasn't. Tristine felt like a failure. Mario promised her that eventually the God he praised, reached out to for comfort and gave all of his heart to would be the same God she'd learn to love in time.

But He wasn't. He was a wall between them, a source of contention. He loved Him more than her and she felt like it was a relationship she would always be on the outskirts of. Dutifully she stood on the sidelines, feeling less like a wife and more like a jealous lover, the guilt of her private thoughts eating away at her.

Mario spent long hours investing in the lives of other people. He listened to them, counseled them and let them cry on his shoulder at all hours of the night. Tristine wanted him to comfort her, be there for her in the middle of the night. How do you compete with God? She frequently asked herself. She felt petty complaining about the calling she agreed to support him in when she said 'I do'. So, instead of sharing her insecurities with her husband, she buried her distress beneath her sadness and went on.

When their daughter, Cameron, was born Tristine thought Mario would lay off the church business and allow her to lose herself in motherhood. She finally had someone to give her heart to, finally had a love that she understood. Tristine felt she'd found her place and purpose in life. In her mind a sort of truce had been parlayed through Cameron. She would let Mario have his relationship and she would have hers. Their cozy quartet (God, Mario, Cameron and she) would live within a series of overlapping bubbles where only Mario and she existed in the middle.

Unfortunately, Mario wasn't content or bound by her silent treaty. The addition of Cameron made Mario even more incessant about Tristine taking her rightful place beside him as a leader of the church. She thought she'd found freedom but in actuality she only felt more boxed in.

She never could understand what all the jumping, hollering, singing and noise were all about. Tristine was brought up in a conservative, reserved Catholic Church and couldn't grasp what having a personal relationship with God was about. To her it was embarrassing. If knowing God meant crying and snotting in front of people you barely knew and opening yourself up to share your feelings and being vulnerable in front of strangers, it wasn't the gig for her. All these believers could have their personal relationship. She'd take a priest and a confessional any day.

The women at Living Waters were a whole other issue. They made sure she always felt like an outsider. She couldn't pull Bible verses out of the sky, or a hat or her ass, as she suspected several of them did. Sometimes, instead of babying the women who came to her for counseling and telling them that with God everything was going to be alright, she wanted to smack them. She wanted to tell them it's not God's fault, it's yours. God didn't make him walk out on you, you did.

Mario told her she had to be nice and gentle and not hurt people's feelings. And time, of course, time would make it all better. Every prayer meeting, Bible study and Sunday service heaped globs of guilt on her shoulders. This life, this walk as they were fond of calling it, was not hers. She'd tried for fifteen years and now she'd had enough. Time was something Tristine had run out of.

| 21 |

Mario came home from afternoon service infuriated that he'd had to make excuses for his wife, again. What'd she expect from him? She wasn't even trying anymore. At this rate her 'migraines' were going to have to turn into brain tumors in order for his members to keep believing him.

He'd already had to deal with Mother Wilson at midday service. She cornered him in the name of good intentions. When she smelled his fear, she brought her claws out, happy to draw blood.

"So, Pastor Fellows, how's your lovely wife doing this Sunday afternoon?"

"She's just fine," he lied. "Her migraines are acting up again. She's at home resting trying to keep the house as dark and quiet as possible."

"Oh," Mother Wilson replied as if she was waiting on this particular response. "Poor thing. Hmm... she's been having a lot of these 'migraines' lately."

"Yes Mother, now that Cameron's growing up I think she's feeling a little stressed. You know how it is these days, trying to juggle so many things at one time."

"That's true. Times aren't like they were in my day when women could focus on their families and homes. Now-a-days they have careers and such to keep them spread out."

"Yes ma'am, times have definitely changed. Well, let me get home Mother and tend to my wife."

"You do that and tell her we'll be praying for her."

"I will. God bless you Mother."

76

Mother Wilson waited until he'd walked far enough away so that when she called his name her voice would carry to the rest of the congregation.

"Pastor?" she paused long enough for him to turn around but started speaking before he'd had time to walk back to where she was standing. "Maybe Tristine should go see a specialist. I don't know if you'll find one that has a cure for what *only* ails you on Sundays, but maybe you'll get lucky." Having made her point Mother Wilson walked away delighted at her successful attempt in making him look like a jackass.

Today was the day Mario would finally put his foot down. After fifteen years Tristine should have herself together. How long did it take? He'd tried everything he could to make her understand how important it was for her to be by his side, to show a united front for their flock and to stand as a testimony not only to marriage but as a symbol of how Christ loved the Church.

Nothing he said seemed to snap her out of her detached indifference to God. When Cameron was born he thought she'd be the glue that held them together and encouraged Tristine to make her relationship with God and him complete. He felt like his wife didn't see the importance in putting God first in their union. It disappointed him that Tristine looked at His Savior as an outsider in their marriage.

Mario had been upfront with Tristine from the beginning. He told her he was called to pastor a church and she seemed proud and accepting of his vision for their life. He wondered sometimes what happened to the woman who fell into his arms when he proposed to her. The memory coaxed a smile across his face.

He remembered her blaming it on clumsiness but he knew that she was shy about her feelings and only wanted him to hold her. And he did. He held her and promised her over and over that he'd never let her go. Mario didn't want to let Tristine go, but he was running out of ideas to help him direct her passions towards something other than Cameron and him.

It almost felt like she was jealous, but Mario dismissed those thoughts as soon as they entered his mind. There was a block, but

Mario couldn't understand what her hesitance stemmed from. After all, weren't they both Christians?

He resisted the urge to cringe from embarrassment when women came and complained to him that Tristine was unfeeling and treated them with contempt. Mario lost count of how many times he begged Tristine to be patient with them and give them time to warm up to her. His desire was for them to know the smart, warm, funny woman he married. Her response was always the same. She constantly threw up in his face that she wasn't going to be phony and be friends with a bunch of busy bodies who only wanted to be in her business.

Mario guided his car into the driveway and decided he was done pacifying her. Enough was enough, he thought as he marched to the front door. They were going to deal with this today. It was time.

He pushed his key in the front door and something in the air made his heart pound deep in his chest. Sweat beaded his forehead as he turned the key. Something was wrong. He couldn't place his trepidation but he knew it was real.

He bowed his head for a quick prayer. God please don't let me walk into this house and find my wife dead or my daughter hurt. Feeling sorry about his thoughts, Mario walked through the door and hastily took inventory of the house. There were no splatters on the walls, no pools of blood on the floor or overturned furniture from a violent struggle. What he found, as he ran from his bedroom to Cameron's pink and purple polka dotted bedroom and back to their family room, was worse than he'd ever imagined. They were gone. Everything he valued was gone. She hadn't even left him a note.

| 22 |

Damian stood outside the small cottage style house with his hands stuck deep in his pockets, studying the white shutters framing the bay window and noticed one was loose. He stared at the fixture slightly askew and thought about what tools he needed to fix it.

"Oh well," he said to no one in particular, "I came this far. What do I possibly have to lose?"

Damian rang the doorbell and listened to the cascading chimes announce his arrival. He could hear someone coming to the door and hoped he hadn't made a bad decision by coming to her house without her knowledge or consent.

"Damian?" Janice asked, from behind the door.

"Yeah Janice, it's me."

On the other side of the door Janice straightened the already neatly laid lapels of her robe and smoothed the wrinkle free folds. She put her back to the door and did a last minute check to make sure nothing was out of place.

"What in the name of God is he doing here?"

"Janice? Janice?"

"Umm, just a minute."

This was a mistake. She's probably in there hiding her pipe. Damian turned around and took a closer look at the rest of the neighborhood; nice houses, manicured lawns, kids playing outside. Looks could be deceiving. *This was definitely a mistake.* Damian pivoted when he heard the door open.

"Hey," Janice managed, smiling weakly and holding onto the door-knob for support.

"Hey."

"Excuse me for not being dressed. I wasn't expecting company."

"No problem." Damian responded, rocking back and forth on his heels. His hands telegraphed his discomfort, becoming tightly coiled fists pushed deep into his pants pockets. "I'm sorry too, for not calling first. I was in the neighborhood and thought I'd stop by."

Cocking her head to the side, Janice let go of the door and folded her arms across her chest. "How'd you know where I lived?"

"Ugh..." Damian knew he was caught. He hadn't thought this encounter all the way through. When he'd gotten the information he hadn't planned on using it. All he wanted initially was to make sure she kept her distance and didn't make trouble for him.

The detective's package had come that morning. He had no explanation for how he'd gotten there. One minute he was standing at his breakfast bar looking at pictures of her grocery shopping, volunteering at a women's halfway house and attending NA meetings. The next minute he was pulling up in front of her cobblestone walkway. It was as if he'd been on autopilot for the past 30 minutes and hadn't come to his full senses until he arrived at her house.

Unprepared and disoriented Damian chose to retreat. "This was a mistake." He admitted out loud. "I never should've come here."

Damian was half way to his car before Janice realized what was happening. "Wait, Damian. It's ok. Don't leave."

Her request was enough to pause him, but not enough to get him to turn around.

"Please?" she begged. "Please, don't go. Come inside."

This wasn't what Damian wanted. Even though visiting her wasn't a conscious plan, now that he was here, he knew it wasn't to see her grovel. They'd both been through a lot. When would it become acceptable to stop paying for the past? Damian said a quick prayer, plastered a smile on his face, and turned to face his mother.

"Well, since you twisted my arm," he joked and bounded back up the walkway.

A swoosh of relief, that she didn't realize she'd been holding, escaped from Janice's chest. His smile was infectious and she couldn't help responding to him playfully, "Get in here boy!"

The cool air felt good to him. Her space was neat and orderly. No signs of the clutter and mess Damian associated with a crack den. He was finally able to relax, and release the tension he held in his shoulders and neck. Gradually, he unclenched his fists, removed his hands from his pockets and flexed his fingers.

"Not what you expected?" Janice teased Damian as she watched his body unwind.

"No," he nodded jovially, "not at all. I don't know what I expected, but it wasn't this."

"You want to look under the cushions, see if you can find any paraphernalia?"

"You're having way too much fun with this," Damian quipped.

"I am, sue me. Have a seat." Janice offered as she sauntered into the kitchen. A nervous giddiness fluttered around in her stomach. "Can I get you anything? Tea, water, juice?"

"You have any coffee?" Damian watched Janice move around the kitchen, opening cupboards, putting water in a violet cast iron teapot and opening a Suga Buga Bear cookie jar.

Janice opened a few more cabinets searching for Damian's request. "I think I have some somewhere. Found it! It's a dark roast, is that cool?"

"It's what I prefer, thanks. Black." Damian leaned back on the couch and closed his eyes for a moment letting his mind wander. He could still see Janice behind his eyelids maneuvering around the kitchen. He was a little boy sitting at the table kicking his feet in the air, anxious for his afternoon treat. His mother leaned down close speaking to him but he couldn't understand the words.

"Damian? Damian?"

When he opened his eyes, Janice was peering down at him.

"You ok?"

"Yeah, I must've fallen asleep."

"You were out for a minute. Are you sure you're ok?" Janice wasn't prepared to take Damian's word about his own well-being. "You even slept through the whistle."

Damian sat up offering a weak excuse, "I'm tired is all."

"Tired, huh? You look worn out to me." Janice placed the plate of cookies and two mugs down on the coffee table.

"I haven't been sleeping all that well," Damian admitted.

"Why not?" she inquired and gestured with her head for him to pick up his cup.

The first sip was as usual, heavenly for Damian. He let the strong flavor settle into him. Something about the intensity centered him and helped him focus.

"Now look who's having too much fun."

"You caught me," he said, taking another healthy swig. "I didn't start drinking coffee until I went to Seminary. With all the late night study sessions caffeine was a must. Along the way I fell in love with the stuff, the darker the better. I swear it's addictive."

When his eyes met hers he realized, too late, the implication of his words. "I didn't mean it like that."

Janice shook her head downplaying Damian's comment. "Don't worry about it. Listen, we can sit around all day with you trying not to say anything pertaining to my past to offend me, but we both know that would be a conversation of few words. What're we going to do, blink at each other?"

Damian covered his mouth to stop himself from spitting out his coffee when Janice started bugging out her eyes and alternating her eyebrows up and down. She continued her mocking facial Morse code until Damian was doubled over with laughter.

"Ok, ok, I get it. The proverbial kid gloves come off starting now."

"Thank you. Cookie? They're oatmeal raisin. Not as good as Cara's, I admit, but I learned from the best."

Damian obliterated over half of the cookie with one massive bite. "Tastes good to me," he mumbled around a mouth full of the sweet treat. "Extra raisins too."

"Well, Cara was a stickler for the rules. She followed that recipe to the letter every time. No nuts, no chocolate chips, nothing. Me? Not so much. I used to sneak you extra raisins when you were a little boy. You would try to smash them into your cookie."

"I don't remember that," Damian said, sobering a bit.

"Yeah well, I guess I can't expect you to be perfect."

Silence filled the room as Damian and Janice worked up enough nerve to say what was really on their hearts. Experience won over youth and Janice was the first to speak up.

"What're you really doing here Damian? Don't get me wrong, I love seeing you. My heart says this could be a great start for us, but my gut says that you haven't settled on how far you want this relationship to go."

Her candidness and sincerity took Damian by surprise. He thought he knew what he wanted to convey before she began to speak. Her openness left him tongue tied. He didn't want to give her false hope but he didn't want to make any promises he couldn't keep either.

"I really don't know what I want. I wish I could tell you I'm committed to us being this fantastic, reunited, Oprah worthy, mother son duo. We can start here, but I don't know where we'll end up."

"I guess that's fair. Here's the thing," she said scooting to the edge of her seat, joining her hands together, using her fingers to accent her point, "I know I may not deserve a lot. And I know that as we go through this process my feelings and pride will be hurt. I expect that. On some level I need that. What I don't want to be is crushed. Hurt I can handle. Crushed, I'm afraid I won't be able to bounce back from."

"Are we at an impasse?"

"Are we?"

Damian was in a tough place. He'd gotten in over his head and he needed a place of refuge. Although it confused him and caught him off guard, he had to admit this place felt safe.

Damian stuffed the remainder of his cookie in his mouth and brushed the crumbs off his hands over the plate. He finished chewing and swallowing before he simply stated, "I'll try."

"I'll take it," she agreed hurriedly, "under one condition."

"Now we're negotiating? Let's hear what you got."

"I only ask one thing. If you feel like this is getting to be too much for you, don't just drop out on me, ok? Let me know. I promise I'll give you your space, for as long as you need."

"I think that's doable. I thought you were going to ask for a kidney or something."

"Baby steps."

Damian gave her a wry smile and drained the rest of his coffee. He tipped his now empty cup up to Janice gesturing for a refill.

"There is the kitchen and the pot. You are no longer a guest. Help yourself."

Damian rose, stretching slowly as he walked into the kitchen to top off his cup. With more concentration than the task required, he poured the black fluid into the wide mug. Weighing his words carefully and praying for grace Damian called out to Janice from the kitchen. "You feel like talking?"

"Isn't that what we're doing?" Janice knew the joking phase of their impromptu visit was over when no biting retort was thrown at her from the kitchen. "About what?"

"About everything," he said making his way back to the living room. "I wanna know the rest."

"I don't know what good any of this will do you, all of this dredging up the past. Why is it so important for you to know every little detail?"

"I'm tired of being in the dark about who I am."

"But you're not. You're who God made you. You don't have to be a product of your environment. You don't have to let the past dictate anything for you."

"Look, there are some things that have happened. Some things I'm not proud of." Standing up to pace, Damian used the time to formulate his thoughts.

"And digging up old dirt is going to fix this problem you're having?"

"Probably not."

"Then what's the point?"

Damian grabbed another cookie before sitting down again. "I need to know who I am. I need to know what I'm capable of."

"Where do you want to start?"

"Begin at the beginning.

| 23 |

"From what I remember about the stories Cara used to tell us, it started with your great-great grandmother Fannie Mae and her momma, Lucy."

"That's a sick family tradition."

"Well," Janice shrugged nonchalantly, "some families eat pumpkin pie for Thanksgiving. We sold-"

"I get it. But, why? Why would Lucy mistreat her own daughter that way?"

"Topaux, Mississippi, where we were born and raised used to be a mining town. Men would come to work for long stretches of time without their families. There wasn't much in the way of entertainment except drinking and trouble. Lonely men and alcohol are not a good mix."

Damian nodded in agreement.

"Lucy lived in a big boarding house, on Brick Lane, with a few other women who worked as maids in the town for some of the wealthy families. The women usually walked home together. Several of them had been attacked by the rowdy men and with no one to protect them they thought there'd be safety in numbers.

One night Lucy was coming home late, alone, from her housekeeping job. The family she worked for was having a dinner party and Lucy didn't leave until early in the morning. Maybe she thought anyone who could be a threat to her would be either passed out or curled up next to a warm body, I don't know.

Some drunken men were stumbling out of a local shot house when they spotted her and cornered her behind a barn. When they were done with her she dragged herself home and somewhere between the bandages and tears the women came up with a plan to never be hurt again."

"So, they decided to be...?" Softened by his mother's pain, Damian searched to find a word that wasn't as offensive as the obvious one floating around in his head.

"Whores." Janice finished for him. "They decided to be whores. According to town lore, they did some pretty good business too, at first."

It was clear from Damian's expression that he was more than a little uncomfortable with Janice's seemingly lackadaisical attitude towards his great-great-great grandmother's business acumen.

"I'm not praising their choices. Especially when we," she said, gesturing with her hands between Damian and herself, "got the ass end of the agreement."

Janice dropped her chin into her chest, wrapped her arms around her midsection and rocked slowly back and forth, willing her beast to sleep with the rhythmic motion.

When she was ready, Janice launched back into her story again, picking up the thread like she'd never stopped.

"Lucy had Fannie Mae and when it was time she started earning her keep like the rest of the women who lived in the defunct boarding house. And so it went from mother to daughter, generation after generation, with everyone falling in line like little ducklings."

"So, just like that? Whoring was passed down from mother to daughter with no thought of change or escape?"

"You believe in generational curses?"

Damian considered Janice's question and studied her face before answering.

"Yeah. I can get with that. Biblically, it's a sound pattern of thought."

"All of us grew up in a state of depravity that was passed down from birth. I'm not sure if any of us knew we could change. I know I didn't. This was our life, our reality, as messed up as it may sound."

"There's a piece of the puzzle missing though."

Janice was hoping he'd let it go with her simple explanation. She should've known he'd be as hungry as she had been to get some insight into their family.

"I mean I understand how Lucy, in her hurt and anger, made a misguided attempt to take back control of her life. To reclaim what had been taken from her on her own terms. Somehow things got switched. How did the family business go from debauchery to torture?"

"Sula."

"And Sula was?"

"Sula was your great grandmother. From the pictures I've seen she was beautiful. She had the smoothest dark cocoa skin and dimples that looked like cherry pits had been stuck in her cheeks. Oh, and she was tall, what they used to call statuesque; all curvy and dense, thick and juicy looking. Like if she walked by you-you couldn't resist trying to take a bite out of her."

Sula's smile surfaced on Damian's face. It was the one feature, despite decades of genetic mish mash that they all shared.

"Don't laugh at me." She admonished him playfully, flashing a little of Sula back at him. "I remember sneaking into Ma Lou's room when she went out and staring at photos of Sula for hours. There was a light and buoyancy about her in all of her pictures."

Janice grew quiet again. They'd been sharing a light hearted moment when the air was sucked out of the room by Janice's memories. Her dark recollections were so oppressive they pushed down on anything good, crushing it under their weight.

"She sounds like a knockout." Damian commented attempting to get them back to a lighter place.

"She was." Janice wrestled with what to tell him next. She was the only one left who could tell this part of their story. Did he need to know everything? There was no unringing of the bell if she let it all out. She bit the inside of her lip until the physical pain transcended her emotional bruises. Her teeth were almost touching through the delicate flesh, the taste of pennies trickling on her tongue before she spoke.

"Cara was twelve when it happened," she stated flatly. "Ma Lou was still living in the big house on Brick Lane with Cara, Peachie and Ruth Ann. Fannie Mae died when Sula was a teenager from some mystery illness women who sell their bodies and don't get regular check-ups are afflicted with. People said she killed herself, but she didn't. Sula was well into her thirties maybe early forties when Lucy killed her."

"Wait a minute. Lucy killed her? Why?"

"Jealousy. Parceling herself out over the years made Lucy cruel and bitter. Cara and Peachie told us how they used to grab Ruth Ann and run into one of the empty bedrooms and hide under the bed or in the back of a closet when they heard her coming. They said she would smack them and tell them they weren't any better than the rest of them and that they couldn't eat for free forever."

"She was jealous of the kids?"

"No, she was jealous of Sula and she hated anything that Sula loved. Lucy was stuck raising Sula when Fannie Mae died. She did the best she could to break her high spirits. Sula was one of those people who took everything in stride. She took all the abuse Lucy heaped on her and somehow was able to shake it all off and still be this radiant, kind person that everybody loved.

When Sula had Ma Lou she spoiled her as much as she could with them living in a place like that. I don't know how Ma Lou got tricked out, but Cara said that in the early days of the big house she remembered Ma Lou being different. Hell, they all practically grew up together. She said Sula would gather all of them up; her, Ma Lou, Peachie and Ruth Ann when she came along, and sing to them. She read them books and played with them on her days off.

Who knows? Maybe that's the reason why Cara stayed in that shack with Ma Lou for as long as she did. She saw a different side of our misery. I don't even pretend to try and understand anymore. It just was what it was."

Damian shifted uncomfortably in his seat. He was finally getting answers to the questions that haunted him about his past. The demons that lurked in the corners of his mind making him feel insecure, unwanted and incapable of love were finally being swept out of their hiding place. He'd thought he'd somehow feel vindicated and justified. Instead his heart ached for these women; women whose bodies bore the brunt of abuse, addiction and neglect.

They were women who'd been broken and discarded by society and themselves. And yet, this woman who sat across from him had struggled and fought to climb out of the pit she was born into and lived. All these years he'd loved and despised her, ached for her and wished for her permanent removal from his memories.

Still he couldn't deny that he was who he was because of who they were, who she was. He lived because they had. He was a product of all of them. That single nugget of truth both hurt and humbled him. No matter how it hurt, he had to press through. He'd opened this wound. He'd applied the pressure necessary for the puss and infection to erupt on the surface of their lives.

"How'd it happen?"

"The day she died Lucy and Sula were having a huge fight in the up-stairs sitting room. They were so loud people were coming out of the rooms to see what was going on. Cara said she was standing in the door of the broom closet; they had to sleep in there on busy nights when all the rooms were being used.

Usually, they were locked in so they wouldn't get out and disturb any of the customers but Cara had stolen a key and ran out into the hallway when she heard all the commotion. When she wiped the cold out of her eyes and could see what was going on, Lucy and Sula were trading blows and curses. Lucy's clothes were torn and one of her eyes was swollen completely shut. Sula had a few little scratches on her but no real damage.

Sula was getting the best of her. Lucy may have been older but she was trying to hold her own. Sula had more to lose though. Lucy was trying to force Ma Lou into making Cara start earning her keep and contributing to the business.

I don't know how long they went at it. I guess Lucy was getting tired because she took a switchblade out of the top of her bra and

started swinging blindly. Everybody was falling backwards over themselves trying to get out of the way. Lucy just swung and swung, twirling
around the room searching for Sula.

Blood was running down into her eyes. The more she moved, the
more she bled. The more she bled, the harder she sliced. Cara said she
was glued to her spot on the floor when Lucy came whirling her way.
She said she saw her coming but she couldn't move. Right before she
was about to cut her, Sula called Lucy's name.

Lucy turned and started working her way back across the room with
Sula's voice as her guide. She wasn't hitting anything and it was pissing
her off. Sula was wearing Lucy down when she accidentally backed herself into the banister. It was all over then. Sula gasped when her back
hit up against the hardwood.

That was the last sound Cara heard Sula make. She didn't even see
the knife stop swinging. All she saw was Sula bent over clutching her
stomach before her knees buckled and she crumpled to the floor. She
fell like a rag doll. Her feet slid from under her while her head lay to
her left side. She was so tall the side of her head almost rested on the
hardwood floor next to Lucy's feet."

Damian was stunned into silence. He slumped into the soft cushions
of the couch, trying to process all he'd learned. Janice let him have his
moment.

"You ok?" Janice asked after a long period of reflection.

"Yeah, I'm cool. Go ahead."

"You sure?"

"I'm sure. I want this," Damian admitted and then corrected, "I need
this."

"So, after-"

"Wait," Damian interrupted. "Where was Ma Lou when Lucy killed
Sula?"

The boy don't miss much, Janice thought to herself.

"Ma Lou was out on a date when Sula was murdered. When she
came home Sula's body still lay in the same heap where she died. Lucy
refused to let anyone move the body. Cara said she tried to run to her

when she fell, but Lucy pointed the knife at her and told her *'you bet not touch her.'*

Peachie and Ruth Ann had woken up by then. The three of them huddled together and watched the dark red circle grow wider around Sula's body. When Ma Lou made it home she ran up the stairs and saw her children lying in one pile and her mother lying in another.

Cara tried to call out to her but Ma Lou shushed her. Well, actually, the slap she gave her shushed her. Ma Lou went to Sula and was met with the same threat that stopped Cara, 'you bet not touch her.' Only it didn't stop Ma Lou from trying to reach Sula.

Lucy raised her foot like she was going to bring it down on Sula's head. Ma Lou stopped then. I don't think she could bear seeing Sula hurt with her own eyes even though I'm sure she had to realize she was already dead. She lay down on the floor stretching her body out as far as it could reach and inched her way towards Sula.

She'd made it to the circle of blood before Lucy let her know that she was serious about her previous threat, except, she didn't stomp on Sula's head. She balanced the ball of her high heels on Sula's temple and made a twisting motion like she was putting out a cigarette."

Unconsciously, Damian gasped and covered his mouth afraid of what might come out next.

"Ma Lou cried like a baby, 'Mama, Mama, Mama,' until she lost her voice. When she couldn't make any sound her fingertips spoke for her, splashing in Sula's blood echoing the rhythm and timber of her silent cries, 'Mama, Mama, Mama'.

Cara, Peachie and Ruth Ann fell asleep to the pitter patter of Ma Lou's fingers speaking through Sula's blood. When they woke up, it was to Ma Lou pulling and yanking on them to get up and move. She half pushed and half pulled them down the stairs. They ran from the big house in the middle of the night, with nothing but the clothes on their back and an old book filled with pictures tucked underneath Ma Lou's arm.

Ma Lou found a tiny shot house out in the country and the rest as they say is history. I was the baby. Ma Lou's craziness was already a part of everyday life by the time I came along. I never saw Lucy and as far as I know she never saw us. We were forbidden from even stepping foot on Brick Lane."

"Don't you ever wonder what happened to Lucy?"

"For, what? I never knew her. All I knew, or cared to know, about her I got from stories passed down through Cara and Peachie."

"For, closure?"

Janice understood it would be hard for Damian to understand her need to keep the past at bay. He was new to the monstrosity her sisters and she fled from and into. She'd lived it every day and knew the dangers of letting it consume you. At some point, she felt, you had to let it go.

"Listen Damian," she began carefully, "we lived like caged animals in that sorry excuse for a home. Our only value reduced to Ma Lou's most basic needs. We had nothing and to her we were nothing."

"But," Damian reasoned, "the fact that she took the pictures shows she was capable of love. Doesn't it?"

"No, Damian." Janice countered. "You don't get it. She left any love she might've had in the Big House. "

"But-"

"That photo album of Sula was the only treasured thing in the entire house. Ma Lou kept it under her mattress wrapped in a silky red cloth covered with tropical flowers. She caught us flipping through it one time. We thought she'd left for the night but she'd doubled back for a scarf and found us in her room.

Cara and Peachie got the worst of it. They tried to shield the rest of us from the beating but Ma was like a mad dog. Foaming at the mouth and barking out crazy stuff. Every so often you could make out *'she's mine, she's mine, give her back'*.

I lost track of the things she grabbed to hit us with. She was relentless. When she finally let up we were a tangle of bodies. We never saw that album again after that."

"She hid it?"

"Doubt it. I think she got rid of it. No, I think she destroyed it. She'd rather lose her one precious thing, than share Sula with us, with anybody."

"She was damaged." Damian made the statement like it was a proclamation.

"Huh?"

"She was damaged," he repeated. "I can't fathom what it's like to be passed around and given away to strangers for money or for sport. I imagine that kind of helplessness makes you need to control whatever you can around you. Makes you destroy the only thing you love so that no one else can possess it or taint it."

Janice's voice rose above Damian's head, "Don't take up for her. Don't make it seem like what she did was right."

"I'm not. Listen, I'm not trying to justify what she did to you, to all of you, but I can see it. I can see it."

"See what?"

"A life."

"Is that all?"

"Isn't that enough?"

| 24 |

"Now, brother?"

"No Maveth. His mind is not yet completely made up."

"But," Maveth interjected, "his bags are packed. Not even the woman and the relationship The Almighty has restored to him has swayed his thinking in this."

"Listen to his heart." Racham instructed.

Maveth and Racham bow their heads in unison. A blinding glow emits from their robes.

"Do you feel Him?" Racham asks.

"Ruach HaKodesh!" Maveth exclaims. "He is still present within him?"

"Does He not reside in all the Master has set apart and sealed?"

Maveth's brow creased as he considered Racham's question in-depth.

"Is it His presence we are measuring before our mission is to be completed?"

"No. Not His presence, but the strength of this one's flesh."

| 25 |

"Good Evening Lakefield I'm Tracy Phillips with WJKZ News your prime source for what's happening in your neighborhood. As we begin tonight's evening news we've got an update on the jaw dropping church scandal that WJKZ broke exclusively just this afternoon. Earlier we gave you an official statement from Senior Pastor Mario Fellows, while 'Circle Scam' masterminds Bishop Anthony Thomas and Junior Pastor Damian Hardwin are still on the run.

As previously reported Thomas and Hardwin cheated well to do members of Living Waters out of hundreds of thousands of dollars. Some couples had even reached into their life savings thinking they were helping to bring the message of Jesus Christ's good works to impoverished communities abroad. WJKZ was able to reach out to the couple who helped blow the lid off the whole corrupt operation. Joining us now are Mr. and Mrs. Dominic Trippler who've agreed to speak to us about their ordeal."

"Mr. and Mrs. Trippler let me first thank you for coming and sharing your story with us. We understand how hard it is for you both to be here."

"Thank you Ms. Phillips," the Tripplers replied in unison.

"Call me Tracy."

"Thank you Tracy. My wife Patricia and I are just happy to be able to tell our side of the story."

"You're welcome and as promised earlier we are joined by our special guest spiritual expert and world renowned author of the book 'Temple Sheeple: How Religion Herds the Masses'."

"Tom?"

"Hi Tracy, just one correction for you on my title, I'm not a 'spiritual expert'. That would imply that there is in fact a 'spirit' one could gather expertise in. What is a spirit, or as Christians like to say 'holy spirit', anyway? It's a ghost! What are ghosts? They are supernatural manifestations of the unexplainable, unrecognizable, overactive and overreaching imaginations of otherwise normal people. I am a 'religion' expert. I study man made religions, their manipulations and their distortions."

"Well Tom we're definitely getting to the thick of things and fast I might add. Please excuse my misnomer."

"No problem, I just want to set the record straight. If you pick up my new book 'The Unrighteous Path of Man and His Mythical Mistakes' you'll get a clearer view of what I'm talking about."

"When does this jewel hit the street?"

"Luckily, you and your viewers won't have to wait long. My new book will hit the shelves next week. As an added bonus, if you go to my website www.whatgod?.net you can check my calendar for a book signing near you."

"That's certainly exciting."

* * *

"He has done the unthinkable, the unforgivable. I will drop him where he stands. Then will he and this dimwitted woman know the truth?"

"Maveth, wait!"

"No, he must die. He shall live after blaspheming Ruach HaKodesh?"

"Leave him. Does his soul not already bear the stench of death? There is another here that we must protect."

* * *

Dominic and Patricia eyed each other during the exchange between the ultra-perky, clearly flirtatious news girl and the handsome over-bearing heathen. They were both having second thoughts but for very different reasons.

Patricia was appalled by Mr. Preshing's beliefs about God. How could he sit there looking and acting all self-important and inflated and say those things about her God? She was a living witness, as her Gram used to say, of what He'd done for her and her family. She only agreed to be on TV because she was angry and hurt. She wanted the world to know how she'd been wronged and get some emotional payback for all that she'd done for Living Water and all that she'd been put through.

She'd left her home church she grew up in to come to Living Waters. It caused a big stink in her family. Cousins, Aunts, Uncles and her own Daddy refused to speak to her for abandoning Antioch Baptist. Living Waters was supposed to be a progressive church, where people appreciated out of the box worship. In her mind they were trailblazers.

They'd joined Living Waters shortly after Pastor Fellows preached his first sermon. The whole town was talking about the new minister and his pretty fiancé. She was tired of Antioch's all day services and old-timey ways. Everyone there had known her since she was a little girl. Patricia could reinvent herself in a new house of God.

Dominic was easy enough to convince. As long as he could get home before kick-off they could go to hell, as far as he was concerned. Over time they became a staple at Bible studies, picnics, revivals and confer-ences. Every Sunday they took their place on the second pew right be-hind Mother Wilson.

As Patricia pondered her trials and sacrifices, it suddenly dawned on her how much she'd learned at Living Waters. How much she'd grown as a believer. She thought about the marriage conference Pastor Fellows had done on Adam and Eve. A story she thought she knew backwards and forwards since childhood was opened up to her in a whole new way. The Holy Spirit convicted her about her relationship with Dominic and for a time she'd grown closer to God than she ever thought possible. Her face grew flush, embarrassed at her abandonment of the bond she'd so earnestly yearned for and sought after. She'd exchanged it for the shallow need to posture and preen for people who could probably see right through her.

She stole a sidelong glance at her husband of 30 years and her heart broke. Their relationship was dissolving and she knew it was the neglect of her spiritual marriage that was the cause. Dominic had always been skeptical of church, church people and their hypocrisy. It wasn't anything that'd happened overnight, but Patricia started to see a change in him. Initially, when he saw how dedicated she was, Dominic began to open up even more.

She'd bullied him into giving away their savings. He warned her that something didn't seem right. When he confided in her that God had spoken to him and as the head of the household he wasn't going to let them go down such a foolish path, she berated him. Patricia made him feel like he wasn't mature enough or strong enough to know what God was saying. Who was he that God would talk to him? Because of her, they went headlong into Bishop Thomas's scam. Dominic had turned on her, Living Waters and God.

The look on Dominic's face spoke volumes. I won't let him win, Patricia thought. Isn't God still God? Doesn't He still sit on His throne? Patricia closed her eyes and tried to clear her head. None of this made sense. She was ready to go. Patricia bowed her head in prayer knowing what she needed to do, but lacking the fortitude to see it through.

Racham and Maveth stood on either side of Patricia.

"God, please?" she prayed silently as tears ran down her cheeks. "Forgive me, give me strength and get us the hell out of here."

"No," Patricia jumped up. Maveth's fire made her skin warm and Racham's gentle touch stilled her rapid heartbeat. "I will not let you sit here and disrespect our God!"

"Patty?!?!" Dominic resorted to her nickname, pulling on her arm, trying to get his wife to sit down. She was doing it again, overshadowing him.

"Don't Patty me. God did not lie to us nor did He deceive us."

"But, Patty."

"No, Dominic I'm telling the truth and you know it. Listen to me." Patricia knelt in front of him. She took her husband's hands in hers and brought them gently to her mouth. She kissed them tenderly and softened her voice. "I wanted to be a big shot. My heart wasn't right and I didn't listen to you. You were right."

Dominic helped his wife stand and held her to him. He pressed her body tightly into his, fighting to control the dam of emotions welled up inside him.

"I'm sorry. Please forgive me?"

Dominic nodded his agreement.

Patricia turned her attention to the so-called expert in this matter. "Mr. Preshing, I know you don't believe in God and I'm not about to stand here and argue with a fool, but I will say this one thing. Romans 4:11 says that every knee will bow and every tongue will confess to God. You might want to reconsider your stance on doing it by force and not by choice."

Dominic and Patricia marched off the set throwing away the battery pack operated microphones and miniscule earpieces as they went.

"Well that was certainly, um something." Tracy commented trying to gain her composure, while inconspicuously signaling for the director to cut to commercial.

Tom sat in silence mulling over Mrs. Tripplers words. He knew that his lot had been cast a long time ago, but somehow this old woman's words had cut him. He blinked back the tears forming in his eyes knowing that this time he'd gone too far.

| 26 |

Thomas opened up his second bottle of whiskey for the day and thought about all the time he'd put into his perfect con. Everything he worked for was gone. He grew up well acquainted with nothing. This was supposed to be his chance to finally get his due.

"Hell," he said, "wasn't no one gonna give it to me. I had to take it. Fuck the meek," he shouted spilling the amber liquid from the crystal tumbler in his shaky hand. Ice and alcohol coated the Tucson styled walls and cherry stained hardwood floors. "I want my inheritance now," Thomas raged.

He thought back to the days when twelve of them barely existed in a sharecropper's shack on old man Davis' twenty-five acre farm in Topaux, Mississippi. Living one on top of the other Thomas never understood how the rest of his brothers and sisters could walk around happy as pigs in slop. The more he thought about it those hogs lived better than him. He knew for a fact they ate more.

* * *

Anthony Thomas hated everything about that pitiful shack and the people who lived in it. He hated the nauseous mineral smell of dirt mixed with the rain water they collected in a barrel on the side of the house. He hated the raunchy smell of sweat soaked skin, the wild musty primal scent that no amount of lye or Borax could free from his nose.

From an early age his only thoughts were how to get out of that shack and as far away from his family as possible. At seventeen he thought he'd had it all worked out when the Right Reverend Babcock's traveling Holy Ghost Revival tent came to his small town. Word had spread across the different counties in all four directions of the wind about Bishop Babcock's tenacity for saving souls and his immense virility.

His mother finally dragged him to the overflowing tent on a Wednesday night. Adept at making excuses and getting his way Anthony had avoided going to the revival with the rest of his siblings earlier in the week. On Tuesday night his mother heard a sermon so powerful about Satan's stronghold. How he used people, people you loved, people who lived in the same house with you, people who ate the food you prepared and slept under the same roof. Immediately her thoughts turned to her middle son. With a new found determination she made her mind up that nothing would stop her from getting him to the tent and saving his soul.

Midway through Wednesday nights service Anthony was plotting what disease he was going to suddenly come down with when he saw his ticket. The collection plates passed down the aisles piled high with denominations he'd never seen before. When one filled up another one quickly took its place. People turned over their hard earned money to the Lord with no hesitation. Every plate made its way out the side flap of the tent. While everyone else was busy stomping, praising and dancing, hands stretched out to the sky, or waists bent low in supplication, eyes brimmed with tears, Anthony was watching the money.

When people poured out of the tent crying and hugging each other thanking God their eternal souls had been saved, Anthony was watching the money.

"Where you going boy?"

"I'm gon' talk to the preacher. I felt something in my spirit and I wanna know if God is talkin' to me."

"Gon' head then baby, take ya time."

* * *

Mrs. Thomas was so happy with her son's revelation that she forgot her earlier thoughts about how the devil must've had a good grip on

Anthony because he didn't even jump up when everybody else was on their feet shouting 'Amen'. When she saw him sitting there pouting she thought he was thinking of the best way to get out of there. His attitude was so bad she almost stopped thanking God for bringing him there and started to get mad.

She often thought why couldn't he be like the rest of them? God knows they didn't have much, but they had each other. Her family was poor and even she hated the stares and whispers they were treated to whenever they went out. She endured though because she knew that she had a husband and children who were grateful, loving and support-ive towards each other.

Everyone, but Anthony. He acted as if they were all beneath them. He never pitched in with the younger ones or helped out his older brothers with the heavy lifting and manual labor that had to be done in order for them to eke out their meager existence. The boy was selfish, willful, lazy and sometimes just downright mean.

She'd almost reached her limit, when the revival came. She'd stayed up countless nights talking to her husband and praying to God about what to do with Anthony. He was starting to infect the rest of the fam-ily with his bitterness and she'd made up her mind that she wouldn't sacrifice the rest of them for the sake of one. Matthew 18:9 said 'and if thine eye offends thee, pluck it out, and cast it from thee'. To her way of thinking, every time she looked at that boy she was 'offended' and it was time for him to go.

So, when he said he wanted to go talk to the reverend about the Holy Spirit her heart softened and she thanked God for changing his heart. She watched him walk towards the front of the tent and turned to walk home with the rest of her brood. Content in the knowledge that God had taken control and it was out of her hands, finally.

* * *

Nobody noticed the seemingly shy boy with his hands in his pock-ets, watching. He watched them while they joked and laughed, hitting each other on the back, congratulating themselves on a good night's take. He watched them as the last man finished off the mason jar of clear homemade brew and cinched the neck of the old burlap sack full of his money.

The older pot bellied man they called Willie staggered away from the rowdy group of men throwing the prize over his shoulder, his gait off balanced by the heavy sack and strong hooch. He whistled a tune he'd heard in a down the way place two weeks ago when they were hustling a small Florida town near Pensacola. Every town they hit it was the same routine. Get the money and get away fast. The car was always parked a mile or two from the tent in whatever woods was close. Bishop Babcock never wanted the people who willingly gave over the last of their already thin earnings to think that they were anything other than poor servants of the Lord.

Preoccupied by the mosquitoes attacking his alcohol drenched pores the portly man was easy to follow. Being a country boy Anthony always kept a knife in his pocket just in case. He never thought when he set out for the revival that he'd have an occasion to use it, but he was glad he came prepared.

What he didn't know was that THEY always followed the money. The Bishop trusted no one and had eyes hidden behind other eyes. Besides, Willie was known to have a problem dipping into the pot for his various vices. Babcock had spared his wife's brother's life once and was waiting for the chance to not be so generous again.

Anthony stepped out of the shadows of the wood line and worked his way around the driver's side of the truck. He matched Willie footstep for footstep on the loose gravel. Willie heard the knife slide into position before he felt its sharp point press near his right kidney.

"Turn around slow, nigga."

Willie turned like a snail.

"Now gimme da sack."

There were two things Willie knew to be true. One, if he gave over that sack he was as good as dead and two, if he gave over the sack this little milk-breath wet eared punk in front of him was as good as dead.

Caring more about the former than he did the latter Willy tried to talk some sense into the boy.

"Look here now, be easy son." Hands up in the air Willie sized Anthony up. Trying to focus on the sharp knife in the shaky hand, he gave it another try. "You don't know who money you messin' wit."

"Naw you don't know who you messin' wit. This here is yo last time. Gimme da sack!"

Liquor gave his mind a courage and steadiness that his legs couldn't translate. Willie charged too far left. As Anthony drove his knife deep into the fat man's gut he heard the click of a rifle.

THEY always followed the money. Randall and Jack, the Bishop's security team had been following the bag, the boy and the man to see how it would all play out. Like two macabre disjoined Siamese twins the two men's bodies moved in tandem.

Willie's blood flowed from the knife and mixed with the piss streaming down Anthony's leg. The bright red ammonia mixture wove its way through the cracks of loosely packed rocks. Willie's body dropped to the ground to meet Anthony's heart. While one laid the other stood, both completely still with wide-eyed unfocused stares.

"Well, well, well Jack. Look what we got us here."

"Whas dat?"

"We got us watcha call two killed birds wit dis here one stone" Randall said.

"Now how's dat?"

"Well to my way a thinking we's got a thief dead and we's got a thief caught. And both of us is got clean hands."

Jack nodded and grinned at Randall's assessment.

"I'm gon' get da Bishop and da Sheriff. We don't need no misunderstandings. Keep dat rifle trained on da boy till I gets back."

| 27 |

"Maveth, do you hear that?"

"I confess I hear nothing over the beating of his evil heart."

"Is it because your ears are not tuned to it?"

"We have no purpose here Racham. The boy has made a choice. Is it our Masters plan to intervene on this one's behalf?"

"No, but was it not the Master who decreed that the prayers of the righteous availeth much?"

Maveth shook his head in confusion. "R-Racham" he sputtered in amazement. "Where is the righteous one here? Is it the boy with the bloody knife, the demon ridden man holding the shotgun or maybe the drunkard lying there in the gravel with his sour smell seeping into the earth? If you point the righteous one out to me will I not help raise his prayers to heaven with a fervor untold?"

"Be quiet and still your fervor brother. Just listen. His mother yet cries out for him. Is this a righteousness that meets your standards?"

Racham did not wait for an answer. He knew what had to be done. "Maveth is it not in your power to touch the sheriff?"

Understanding immediately Maveth let the fringes of his righteous anger reach out to touch Sheriff Jones.

| 28 |

Sheriff Jones ran a two and a half man operation. It was him, Grayson "Micro" Mitchell and a worthless piece of crap everybody called "Bubba" Lawson. He'd been saddled with Bubba for the past eight years. When his best friend, Lucky, died in the war he promised both their mommas that he would help take care of his only son Bubba.

Bubba's mom left when he was just three weeks old. Mary Jo and Seymour, Bubba's grandparents, were good law-abiding Christians, but they spoiled that boy something awful. If he'd known what a thorn Bubba would be in his side, Billy Ray swore he would have drowned him at birth himself.

When the Lawson's came to him, reminding him of his declaration of responsibility and his neglect, he had no choice but to give Bubba a job. It took two days for Billy Ray to figure out that everything he'd heard about the boy was true. Bubba became his glorified errand boy with the undeserved title of Junior Deputy Sheriff with no chance of or motivation towards promotion.

Billy Ray felt like he was a fair man of the law. He was a big man. He stood 6'6" on flat feet, with a head as big as a Brahma bull and fists the size of two newborns. Billy Ray was an imposing figure but he tried not to rely on his size to solve any issues that common sense could weigh in on. He didn't allow any of the foolishness that other towns dealt with. Anytime a group of liquored up crackers rolled up to his line in the sand he told them nicely to head back to where they came from. If they chose not to listen he'd let the buckshot speak for him.

It wasn't that he was especially partial to the Coloreds, but they'd developed a tolerable relationship over the past ten years he'd been in office that all parties were comfortable with. They left the good White people of Topaux to their own affairs and he left them to theirs. The only time he intervened was when there was a work dispute of some sort, but that was rare.

He let the Coloreds handle their business through his liaison of sorts, Deputy Mitchell, known mostly by his nickname Micro. Micro was the only Colored official in the whole state of Mississippi. Billy Ray caught a lot of flak for his appointment, at first, but nobody would argue that when Micro spoke people tended to listen.

He was the exact polar opposite of Billy Ray. Only 5'2" in boots, Micro didn't look like he was much to deal with. He had a little muscle to him, but his biggest assets were his speed and his strength. Everybody knew he could out lift Sheriff Jones pound for pound any day. Nobody talked about it, but everybody knew.

Sheriff Billy Ray Jones had hoped that Bishop Babcock's traveling circus of horseshit would skip his small town and head for somewhere bigger like Biloxi. Reports had been coming in all month from up and down the coast about the slick drifters conning small town folk out of their money. He'd just gotten off the phone with his cousin Tommy Boy in Littletop, Florida warning him about the chaos that was sweeping through his neck of the woods.

To hear Tommy Boy tell it Babcock had caused enough drama to keep his jail cells near to overflowing with cussing, cutting, fighting folks for the past three weeks. The poor people's coffers weren't the only thing Babcock and his crew was fond of dipping in. Bellies were blowing up from Lower Chiptaw to Appalache County.

Billy Ray was all set to let this whole Babcock mess go before he got the call from Tommy Boy. He knew it was their last night in town. He'd sent Bubba down there at the beginning of the week to tell him he had three days to do all the Bible thumping, jumping and hollering he wanted to do. But, the fourth day better not find him and the city of Topaux rising underneath the same sun.

Something kept nudging and pushing at him. The longer he sat thinking about it the more agitated he got.

"Bubba!"

"Yeah Sheriff" the Junior Deputy said, unhappy about being startled out of his nap.

Billy Ray shook his head at the lazy bastard. Why those wooden legs hadn't bent under the pressure of all that weight he'd never know. They made him give him a badge, he'd be damned if he'd ever give him a gun.

"You seen Micro?"

"Naw, I think he went down to Tweela Bird's for supper."

Sheriff Jones stared dumbfounded as Bubba started to return to his nap. For a large man he could move as quiet as a cat. No small feat due to the creaky boards that made up the old floor. Billy Ray kicked the chair from underneath Bubba and sent him sprawling to the floor.

"GET THE HELL UP AND GO GET 'EM!"

Bubba took a minute to adjust himself. He blinked his pig eyes up at Billy Ray trying to make his mind register why he was no longer asleep and how he ended up on the floor.

"Boy I ain't but two seconds off ya. Get up, go down to Tweela's and tell Micro we fissin' ta ride."

Bubba meandered out of the office and headed south towards the popular Colored eatery.

"Jesus H. Christ. I shoulda sent that boy wit a note to have Tweela put me something in a bag, that gal can go to town on a poke chop sandwich."

| 29 |

Randall ran through the thick woods with branches slashing at his fair skin. Tomorrow he'd look like he'd been fighting with a gang of squirrels. He couldn't afford to worry about that tonight. Tonight he had to get back to Bishop Babcock before anybody saw the dead man in the woods.

He hoped to find Babcock giving last minute instructions for the next spot since it was their last night. They'd only spent three nights in Topaux where they usually spent seven. Randall was contemplating cutting his losses after the next two or three towns. This revival business had been a good long con, but he felt like their good luck was running out.

* * *

Before their caravan could get the pegs into the site of their newest holy ground some big stupid looking redneck Junior Deputy had shown up with a message from the local sheriff. It spooked the hell out of some of the men. They weren't used to the law meeting them at the door. In most places, if they saw them at all, it was towards the end of their stay with palms sunny side up waiting to be greased.

The men smiled big tooth baring grins despite the uneasiness they felt as Bubba toggled back and forth, making his way through the camp site. Mac and Big John quickly removed their newsboy hats and bowed their heads in submission. Rico kept his relaxed stance, leaning on the hood of his light blue GMC pick-up, but his jaw clenched with tension.

"Look here boys," Bubba drew the last word out looking for a reaction from the men.

"Yes suh?" Babcock replied hat in hand. Playing the role of the submissive Negro made his insides boil. He was careful to make his voice drip pure molasses instead of the venom he felt building up in his incisors.

"I gots a message to deliver from the Sheriff. Y'all boys better not be lookin' inta any trouble round these parts. Our niggers are good and wholesome. They don't take too kindly to folks comin' up in here an' mixin' thangs up!"

"Naw suh." Randall joined in the rouse. "We ain't aiming fa no trouble. Onliest mixin' we doin' is from sinnin' to saint."

"Make sure them saints is mixed up good in three days, else you gon' have me to contend wit'."

Bubba extended himself up to his full height, and pulled his utility belt high up on his waist, trying to display his superiority over the men. He knew he'd taken it too far when he put his hand where his pistol should've been and rested his palm on his standard issue flashlight. He swallowed repeatedly hoping to remoisten his mouth as Babcock eyed him suspiciously.

He took a good look at the men and counted three shotguns and four pistols he'd neglected to see when he entered the revival grounds, throwing his weight around.

A menacing smirk danced across Babcock's face. Babcock gave the oversized Junior Deputy a deep bow, exaggerating his movements. "Yes suh. Three days. Thank y'all good folks ever so much."

Embarrassed by his fear Bubba unhinged his flashlight as he turned to walk away from the men and broke out the tail light of Rico's truck.

"Betta' get dat fixed for y'all get," Bubba grinned, reasserting his dominance before leaving the men.

Rico sprang up from his truck. Babcock drew his hand up and signaled for the angry man to settle down.

"Fat bastard done tore up my light." Rico spat a long glob of tobacco on the dusty ground.

"It ain't worth it," Babcock cautioned. "I know it don't seem possible, but we gots bigger fish ta fry. Let me lay it out for ya."

Babcock worked his magic and smoothed things over with the skittish men. He gave them a rousing speech about David and Goliath and standing up to your enemies in the face of adversity. Randall had to give it to him, all of the men knew what kind of man Babcock was, but that snake's tongue was so quick and slick he could make them believe anything.

Randall had been with Babcock since they were teenagers sliding wallets in St. Louis. He knew what the man was and most importantly he knew what he could do. When the smoke cleared Babcock would be long gone and everybody else would be left holding the bag. Not him and not this time.

That not so subtle threat was Randall's sign that their reputation was preceding them. Not good at all when the plan was to ride into town as saviors. They relied on an air of mystery. Their shtick was showing up just in the nick of time with the revelation of the word and its miracles. It made them seem heaven sent and made it easier for the locals to hand over their money as alms for their unexpected blessing.

* * *

Randall raced up to the semi-broken down tent perspiration pouring into his eyes making it hard to see. His skin burned and itched where his sweat dripped into the cuts and scratches left from the assault by the branches. In the back of his mind he prayed he wouldn't have to go find Babcock in some errant country girl's bed.

"Hey, Lou?"

"What's up man?"

"You seen Babcock?"

Lou stopped hammering one of the large shipping crates and gave him a knowing smile. "Man you know the time. It's like clockwork."

Randall gave him a look that said he was not in the mood to play games or talk all around the mulberry bush.

"Alright" Lou said. "I seent him wit' some fine big boned gal 'bout a hour ago. She was lookin' like she was hungry and he was lookin' like he was ready ta eat."

"Make it plain Lou. I'm losin' my patience. Where she stay?"

"Man, how the hell I'm 'posed to know? You come struttin' up on me all swole askin' me a bunch of damn questions and then get mad. Man, fuck you! I got shit ta do!"

"Look Lou, we got trouble and we gon' have some more if you don't tell me where that gal stay. I don't have time to babysit ya hurt feelins." Randall took out his switchblade and pointed it towards Lou. "Now either you spill it or I spill you, take ya choice nigga."

"Be cool baby, be cool." Lou said, his arm hanging loosely at his side, fingers clenched tight around his hammer. "I tole you they was gon' ta eat, bunch of 'em went down ta Tweela's. You know dat's da only place a transplant nigga can get somethin' ta eat dis time a night."

Randall turned and headed down the hill to Tweela's without a word of thanks to Lou. He could hear him screaming after him.

"And kiss my ass too, nigga. Hey, hey, bring me back one a dem poke chop sandwiches."

Randall ran as hard and as fast as his weary legs would carry him. Time was moving faster than his feet could pound the dusty road. He vowed that if that fool Lou made him miss Babcock he was going to double back and gut him anyway.

He halted in mid stride when he saw the Junior Deputy resting on the bottom step of Tweela's. He knew the fat man was a staple there, but he'd only seen him during the day. Not too many 'other' folks came into the Colored parts of town at night. Randall stepped into the shadows and waited. He couldn't risk going into the restaurant now, there was too much at stake.

| 30 |

Bubba stopped at the bottom step of Tweela's to catch his breath. He hadn't been moving that fast but it took effort to move all 350 pounds of him in any direction. The thought of food always made his blood pump a little faster and the thought of Tweela's food made it pump twice as fast.

Winded, Bubba finally hauled himself up the two steps to Tweela's front door. He could hear the nigger music from the street. If there was anything he envied the niggers for it was their food and their music. Being an upstanding White Christian man he'd never admit that out loud, but it was the truth. The brothers at the Klan house already gave him a hard time about how much he ate down here. They poked fun at him and told him how he was going to turn into a darkie one day while secretly sliding him two dollars to bring them something back.

If he'd been sent any other place besides Tweela's he would've been mad. He didn't know why he had to come all the way down here to get Micro. Hell, it wasn't like he wasn't going to come back after supper.

The moment Bubba stepped into Tweela's, mouth's stopped mid chew, laughter ceased and eyes cut in his direction without directly staring. Micro could feel the shift in energy before he looked up to see the cause. *Something serious has got to be up for Bubba to drag his carcass up from the sheriff's office all the way down here*, he mused. He motioned for Tweela, at the bar, to wrap his supper up to go.

"Micro," Bubba shouted from across the room on his last good breath. "Billy Ray said get on back to the station."

Micro kept his seat and trained his eyes on Bubba's blotchy red face, through the mirror facing him on the opposite wall. This was going to become a test of wills where both parties already knew the outcome.

"Micro? You hear me boy?"

Micro focused his attention back to the evening paper and drinking his coffee, slowly. Bubba knew better than to come to his neck of the woods and try to show out, but some people learned their lessons the hard way. Micro's years in the Army had taught him that the best way to deal with Bubba's brand of ignorance was to ignore it.

As soon as 'boy' slipped from his lips Bubba knew he'd made a big mistake. Now, everyone was watching him to see how he would react to Micro not reacting to him. He had no choice but to wind his massive hips through the tables in the crowded dining area. People over exaggerated their *hey's* and *watch out man's* as they grabbed glasses and protected overflowing plates, adding to his chagrin.

When Bubba finally bumped his way over to Micro's booth, he still didn't get any attention. Micro decided he wasn't in the mood to meet anyone halfway tonight. Bubba stood watching him drink coffee and turn pages for two agonizing minutes.

"Micro?"

"Hmm?" Micro said, still staring at the newspaper.

"Sheriff wants you to come back to the office." Bubba leaned in, careful to keep his voice down.

Without looking at Bubba, Micro picked his head up and gave Tweela a nod signaling it was time to bring his bag and took another long slow sip of coffee. You could almost see the smoke starting to gather around the edges of Bubba's ears. His face read like a human thermometer as color rose up his cheeks.

Micro reached into his back pocket searching for his wallet, still refusing to acknowledge Bubba. Tweela sashayed over to the table and set down the big greasy paper bag she'd been holding with both hands. Bubba had to stumble out of the way to make room for her and the bag.

Tweela wasn't one for saying excuse me in her own establishment. People had a tendency to look at her diminutive frame and think she'd be a pushover, but Tweela Mae Wiggins never let anyone push her anywhere. She had the presence of a 4-star general and the diplomacy and charm of a master negotiator.

"Here you go, Micro."

"Thanks, Twee. What I owe you?"

"My name is Twee-la, Micro Grayson. And I 'spect you'd know that by now," she teased. Tweela pushed a lock of long raven colored hair behind her ear that managed to escape her hairnet.

Micro treated her to one of his sultry grins. "Well, Miss Twee-la, I 'spect you know by now that I like callin' you Twee. It fits you."

Tweela threw her head back and produced a lusty laugh just for him. Her body bent towards his, unmasking the love she was too scared to reveal. She swatted Micro on his arm while he attempted to duck and pretend that it hurt.

"But," Micro continued, "since I don't make it my business to offend the cook, Twee-la it is."

Micro opened his wallet and started to fish out a few dollars. Tweela placed her hand over his lovingly with a discrete stroking motion.

"Your money ain't' no good here. You know that." Tweela cooed, her tone matching her movement on his hands.

Tweela sashayed from the table, shooting longing glances at Micro over her shoulder. Bubba's temperature moved from his cheeks to the top of his overgrown eyebrows. Micro still drank his coffee, waiting for the smell of Tweela's homemade gravy, to permeate Bubba's nose from the pork chop sandwiches in his bag. When he could feel the heat radiating from Bubba's body, Micro figured he'd had enough, for today.

"Sat." Micro said extending his arm to the spot directly across from him. It confused Bubba. He didn't know if he should be offended at the command when Micro's body language made it seem like an invitation.

With tremendous effort Bubba got half of his right leg and an eighth of his gut behind the table on the other side of the booth. Micro knew he wouldn't fit, but he figured it was a sure way to get the fat man to hurry up and spill what he'd come to say.

"What?" Micro said, finally looking into Bubba's eyes.

"Sheriff said you need to come on back cuz he's in a tizzy about something with the nig-coloreds and he said y'all fissin' ta ride," Bubba gushed in one huge breath. The booth was crushing him and he was ready for this whole ordeal to be over.

Micro eyed him and tried hard not to bust out laughing at Bubba's big behind steadying himself on the edge of the seat. His left leg was already cramping from putting extra weight on the bench so he wouldn't go flying in the air when Bubba was squeezing into the other side. He thought about standing up fast just to see him fall to the floor, but he decided that would be petty. His aim was to make Bubba treat him with respect, like a man. He wasn't trying to humiliate him the way Bubba had tried to do him.

"Alright, let's go." Micro grabbed the paper sack and timed his getting up with Bubba's grunts and shoves. When they made it outside Bubba was looking at Micro's bag like there was something in it for him. Micro had gotten two extra sandwiches intending to give one to Bubba when he returned from supper, but his pride wouldn't let him reward the man for his callowness. He'd give both sandwiches to the sheriff, if he wanted to share them that was his business.

Micro took a lengthy sidelong glance at Bubba standing there drooling. He changed his mind, maybe he did want to humiliate him. Micro took off running North, up the hill to the sheriff's office. He didn't slow down until he stopped hearing Bubba's labored breathing and heavy footsteps.

| 31 |

Randall had to chuckle to himself when he saw the fat man try to run after the Colored deputy. No way, in a million years, would he catch up to him. That Colored fella better be careful; if he catch em, he bound to eat em.

He hadn't seen anyone from the gang come or go out of Tweela's while he was hiding in the shadows. If he was lucky Babcock would still be inside with the girl if they'd ever been there at all.

Randall did a quick scan of the room when he entered Tweela's. No Babcock, but some of the boys were sitting in the rear by the kitchen near the backdoor.

"Hey fellas, you seen Babcock?" Randall asked as he reached the table.

"Man," Johnson said, cocking his head to the side, "you don't hear em?"

The whole table broke out in grins and hand slaps at their private joke.

Randall took a few steps in the direction Johnson motioned and heard deep moans before his hand reached up to push on the backdoor. He stepped into the backyard and caught Babcock in mid stroke. He barely missed a beat when he looked up to see Randall standing there gawking.

The girl looked like she couldn't have been a day over twelve complete with pigtails, bobby socks and Mary Janes. She was built like a woman, but her face and eyes told a different story. He could see her innocence slipping out of her as Babcock was forcing his way in. The thought of his little girl being held up and rammed into behind some greasy joint surrounded by trash cans made his body tremble. *Keep yo head*, he cautioned himself. *Won't be long, bastard gon get his.*

"Stop, he lookin'," she squealed and begged, trying to get Babcock to put her down.

"Hush now," Babcock pleaded between thrusts. "He's my friend. He don't mean you no harm. Ain't I here to protect you? Ain't I fed ya and taken care of ya?"

The young girl, her body at war with the excruciating pain and involuntary pleasure, playing havoc with her senses, could only shake her head in agreement. Randall turned his back and held back tears telling himself this wasn't his problem or his fault.

"Babcock finish up we got to go!"

Randall's tone made him stop. All of the men knew to call him Bishop when they were around other people. Something dropped into his bowels and made him flaccid. He put the girl down, gave her his handkerchief to clean off with and a crisp $10 bill he plucked from the gold money clip in his trousers.

"Tell your momma I said thank you for her contribution to the kingdom. Blessed are the handmaidens that facilitate the way of the servant of the Lord."

Babcock pulled off another new $10 bill for good measure and patted her on her head.

"This one's for you," he winked.

| 32 |

Iridescent silver liquid oozed from Maveth's pores as his anger called to his armor. The illuminated dots ran together, hardened and formed the protection Maveth wore when he was summoned into war. A breastplate, with an open mouthed lion, appeared on his chest. Scale armor emerged on the surface of his shoulders and forearms. Greaves adorned his shins and a coat of mail wrapped itself around his waist.

The sickle sword that typically hung in its leather holder on his left side manifested in his right hand. A light shot out from the palm of his left hand and rotated clockwise forming a large metallic shield encrusted with sardonyx, malachite, jasper and lapis lazuli. His eyes went beyond their ferocious blue fire and transformed to white ice.

Racham stood stoic and still, watching Janice clean herself while the two defiled men made their plans. Salt caked cheeks were all that was left of his tears. Unlike his brother, Racham was intimately acquainted with the evil men harbored in their hearts. He was there at the First Fall and remembered the raw stench of sin. Despite his familiarity, violations against the defenseless still had the ability to torment him.

"Brother, stay your hand."

"Racham, you have the ability. His mercy. What about His mercy?"

"His mercies, His vengeance, do they not all belong to Him to dispense as he pleases?"

"So we do nothing?" Maveth asked, even though he knew the question would not be answered.

"Brother, were our instructions not identical? He was clear on this, with no room for movement within His will. It is what He has allowed, not what He has desired. His reasons are His alone."

Maveth calmed enough to retract his weapon and gear. "My gifts are unlike yours. I do not ask out of a need for rebellion or disobedience. You know the Father has not fashioned me in that way."

"This I know, Brother." The two stood as sentries with guarded eyes as the young girl slipped into darkness. When she was out of sight, they turned their attention to the two men left behind.

"His justice will be swift."

Without a backwards glance Racham turned to leave. "We cannot help the littlest one tonight, Maveth. Let us go."

| 33 |

Neither Babcock nor Randall paid any attention to the girl as she reached between her legs with the freshly laundered monogrammed cotton. No one noticed as she limped out of the yard leaving behind two crisp $10 bills, a blood streaked handkerchief and her soul.

Janice knew Ma Lou would be mad about the money, but she didn't care. All she'd wanted was something to eat besides the pinto beans, grease sandwiches, bulldog gravy and sugar water she was forced to call meals. She thought she was the lucky one when he chose her.

Since she was a little girl she'd seen her sisters go off and come back with a full belly and a little change for momma. She'd thought her sisters were just trying to make her feel better about being left out when they dragged their half dead bodies in the house late at night. She thought they were secretly making fun of her when they said 'Naw bay sis, this ain't for you.'

Even Macie Jean got to go out and she was slow. All she did was sit and stare. Even when you clapped your hands in front of her face or snapped your fingers by her ear, she just stared. Ma Lou even made a big deal when it was her turn. She dressed her in a long white gown and put extra powder on her face. Mr. Parsons, one of the body cleaners for the funeral home, would pick her up every Wednesday night at six o'clock and be back exactly one hour later. Janice didn't understand how Macie Jean got to be so lucky before her. After all, who would want to eat with a dummy?

One night after she whined and begged enough Ma Lou looked her over with an eagle's eye, spit juice from the snuff she always held between her lower lip and gums into her cup and told Janice, "You 'bout ripe. Don't worry next time it be you." She was so happy thinking about all the good food she was going to eat; it never crossed her mind why she needed to be 'ripe' to eat it.

* * *

Cara was the only one who didn't go out any more. Peachie, Ruth Ann, Eddie Pearl, Macie Jean and Janice were sitting on the porch try-ing to catch a break from the heat and a breeze from the wind when they heard an ear piercing scream. Janice felt her heart rip in two. She jumped out of the old wobbly wicker chair and tried to run into the house but Ma Lou beat her to the screen door, holding it out while she tried to push in.

"Whatchu want?"

"What's wrong wit' Cara?" Janice was almost in tears thinking about what terrible thing was happening to make her oldest sister make that type of sound.

"Nuttin' she gettin' scraped is all."

"Scraped?" Janice questioned. She'd scraped her knee before, when she tripped playing hopscotch. It felt like the devil was pissing on it, but all she'd had to do was grit her teeth real hard and waive her hand back and forth over it real fast to make it stop burning. She didn't scream like a banshee. Getting scraped, she thought, couldn't be that bad.

"Yeah, scraped. Now get ya lil narrow hips back on the porch till we gets cleaned up in here." Raising her voice so the rest of the girls could hear her, she warned, "Member dis next time one a you gets to thinkin' you too good to drink the tea. I ain't helping ta bring no more nappy headed bastards in this house leeched on to the teat. It make ya titty hang and can't nobody eat like that."

The girls listened to Ma Lou's worn down house slippers shuffling across the dusty floor. "Peachie, you up tonight, since Cara done messed herself up.", she yelled back towards the screen door. "Clevon be here any minute."

Peachie started to make an excuse but couldn't think of anything good fast enough. "But I-I-I ain't hungry," she finally sputtered.

"Make no difference," Ma Lou spat "he is. Just touch up ya hot spots. Clevon ain't particular and he don't take long to eat. Make sure you get an extra $5 since y-y-you ain't hungry" she said mocking Peachie.

* * *

Now Janice knew.

She knew why Peachie cried by herself in the outhouse when she thought no one was listening. She knew why Eddie Pearl stayed out by the rainwater barrel with a torn rag rubbing herself with lye soap until her skin was bleeding, red and raw. Why Ruth Ann was always getting knocked upside the head for showing her stuff behind the Burcher mausoleum in the White cemetery, for free. She knew now the bigger sin was the fee and not the fun.

Tears fell freely when she thought about how Macie Jean found that place inside of herself and never came out. Maybe she wasn't born like that. After what she'd gone through tonight Janice wondered if Macie's first time hadn't been too much. If she could find some hole, real or imagined, to crawl into, Janice promised herself she'd never come out, just like Macie.

The dull ache between her legs was starting to become a burn from the tearing and swelling Bishop Babcock's probing caused. Her pain made only a few short steps bearable at a time. Sweat beaded up on her forehead and started to collect on her upper lip. Janice heard an engine in the distance and turned to see headlights coming down the road in her direction.

She thought about her sisters, Ma Lou and the other kids at school. She thought they laughed at her because her family was poor and known to rotate clothes between all three younger girls during the same week.

Now she knew.

They laughed because they were whores. They laughed because when she told them one day she was going to go out into the world and have fancy dinners like her sisters, they knew she was going to get her cat stretched out, just like her sisters.

Her mind pushed vivid scenes before her eyes like an automatic View-Master. Her thoughts alternated between cruel laughter and the Bishop's hands and mouth on places that made her cringe. Each memory made her inch closer and closer toward the middle of the road. The driver would never see her standing there when he came around the corner. She imagined herself flying through the air, free.

Her heart overflowed with regret watching the Sheriff's backlights move off into the distance. The last half mile was a blur. Janice stood in the front yard for what seemed like hours. She could see Ma Lou sitting in her rocking chair waiting for her cut. Janice opened the screen door quietly hoping small slow movements would help soothe Ma Lou's greedy beast. She stood as far away from the rocking chair as she could in the cramped space head bent in humility and shame.

"You eat good?"

"Yes'm" Janice's voice was barely audible.

"You got what's mine?"

Janice pushed her chin further into her chest willing herself to appear humble if not humiliated.

Ma Lou spat and sat stock still in her chair waiting for an answer that wouldn't come easy. The silence from her previous rocking sucked all of the air out of the front room.

"If'n I has ta ask you again, you gon' mo than regret it."

Out of the corner of her eye Janice could see Cara standing in the doorway of the kitchen miming instructions to be strong and not cry.

"No ma'am" Janice whispered. Her shoulders heaved and her body shook while fresh tears wet the front of her dress. The last thing she saw before the stars and night was Cara's face, mouth formed in a perfect 'o' as she hit the floor.

| 34 |

Micro Grayson jogged up the road clutching the treat from Tweela's close to his chest, barely out of breath. Sheriff Jones stood leaning against the post of the one room structure waiting for the Deputy. He slowed down to a swift walk as he neared the building.

"Where's Bubba?" Sheriff Jones quizzed Micro as he came closer.

"Back there a ways," Micro said, gesturing towards the dirt road.

Sheriff Jones shook his head in disgust and moved the overworked toothpick in his mouth from side to side trying to fight his mouth into submission. The thought of Bubba having nothing to eat but Micro's dust was almost too much to contain.

"Well, hell, I ain't got all night to wait on his fat ass. Let's go."

"Yep, Sheriff. Lemme change my uniform first." Micro held his shirt out where the grease from the paper sack had seeped into his perfectly starched top. He held the bag out to the Sheriff as he walked into the jailhouse.

"Here, I brought you a sack back."

Sheriff Jones took his gift and stuck his whole head into the spotted bag, inhaling deeply. He crumpled the top of the back down tight afraid Bubba might show himself on the road with his mouth open. He hurried into the passenger side of the truck and mentally urged Micro to hurry the hell up.

Micro sauntered over to the truck looking like he'd just gotten dressed for the day. It wasn't too often the Sheriff allowed him to drive. He was a man who liked to be in control of everything. Sheriff Jones never relinquished anything without a fight. The fact that he'd willingly sat in the passenger's side made Deputy Grayson tighten his muscles in anticipation.

"Where we headed?"

"Round the way, through your parts."

"Dat so?" Micro eyed the Sheriff suspiciously through the partially open window.

Micro didn't like making forays into his neck of the woods on official police business without knowing exactly why. He'd built up a strong system of respect and trust in and out of his uniform with the people in his community. They knew he was a man of God and his word was as fair and equal as a man in his position could be. He knew the relationships he'd worked so hard to forge would be destroyed beyond repair if he let Sheriff Jones go after his neighbors half-cocked.

Sheriff Jones eyed Micro when the Deputy's hand paused on the door handle without getting in. *Damn it*, he cursed silently, *every time we go into the Colored side Micro gets his dander up. Hell, I'm the Sheriff with the Coloreds and the Whites.* He blew his breath out in exasperation as the two men concentrated on each other to see who would blink first.

| 35 |

Sweat found its way into Jack's eyes even though the wind blew a crisp breeze through the clearing. The salty fluid irritated him past the point of caring about anything Randall or the Bishop had to say about the situation. He flexed his right thigh, felt his package and let his mind drift to the quiet spot he would find after they got here.

"Shoot, they better come on," he declared. "I could kill this lil piss ant, take the cash and be gone before anybody gets back. First, I gotta get my stomach right."

He flexed his right thigh again and let his mind float.

All Anthony heard was kill, cash and gone. His stomach somersaulted and he hoped the jittery gun man wasn't talking about him. The pee from his earlier bout of panic had made his pants stick to his legs. The night air was making him cold and the smell of the dead man's excrement wafted downwind. Maybe he could convince him to split the cash and they could both get out of here with a little weight to their pockets. Anthony discarded the thought almost as soon as he formed it. He had to find a way to get all the cash or die right now standing on his own two feet.

| 36 |

Racham knew the man with the gun was getting antsy. He knew the man put things in his veins that were not of God. He could feel the longing Jack had for the little ball wrapped in cellophane that he kept in his front pants pocket. He could see Jack's mind filled with thoughts of the little ball.

Jack imagined the feel of his belt wrapped around his bicep. He imagined the sizzle pop sound of the ball cooking on the misshapen spoon he kept in his left shirt pocket near his heart.

Racham cried out when the man's mouth watered at the thought of release from the dirty rusted needle he would stick into the bulging vessel of his track marked arm.

"Maveth, hurry, this one grows weary. I can smell his sickness. It consumes him with a mighty thirst. What if he does not heed his friend's words?"

"Have we not dangerously skirted the edges of the Master's instruction enough? We are not to intervene. This is not the one we were sent for Racham!"

"I of all people know the law, but-"

"But, what? I love the Master above all things" Maveth's eyes turned to black coals flickering hot blue flame. "I WILL NOT JOIN LEGIONS WITH THE ONE WHO HAS FALLEN!"

"How do you accuse your brother of such a thing? Search my heart. Taste and see that it beats for the Master and no other. Does it not still keep time with the celestial beings?"

Maveth did as his friend requested. The flames receded, but his eyes remained like coal. "I find no fault in you brother, but listen to what I speak. It is the truth and spoken from true knowledge and not of that which is learned."

"You have my ear."

"Before The Fallen One left His favor forever, he came to me pumped up with pride and self-fulfillment. He tested my position and lost. Hear me closely. You're nature is that of the Lamb that was slain; your compassion formidable. Do you not twist it with pride when you think that your plan is better than the Master's?"

Racham let Maveth's words seep into him. "I am wrong. The Master's commands are correct above all leanings. I have been here with these humans too long."

"The reason we are two brother. His mother wails for him, stronger now. Ruach HaKodesh speaks to her; they both intercede on his behalf. What would you have me do?"

"Do what the Master would have done.

| 37 |

Sheriff Jones felt the same surge of unexplained anger he'd experienced earlier. This time it was mixed with a sense of impending danger. The truth was he respected Micro. In his heart he believed that Micro felt the same. All the man was asking for was that respect.

Micro saw the look change in Sheriff Jones eyes. He felt his intent in his gut and knew this wasn't the time to have a pissing contest, just because he was feeling territorial. He conceded, settled his spirit with a quick prayer and climbed in the truck.

Jones forgot about the small man's stature until they rode in the pick-up and Micro was driving. The front seat moved as a unit causing his knees to shove into his chest when Micro adjusted the seat to fit his feet on the pedals.

He started to tell Micro to switch, but it wasn't going to be a long trip and those pork chop sandwiches were calling his name. Micro had brought back two; he hoped he wasn't supposed to save one for Bubba. If he was, tonight was not the fat man's lucky night.

Micro made a hard right back in the direction he'd just run from. They rode in silence both men entrenched in their own thoughts. Micro wondered if he should offer some sort of apology or explanation for his behavior, but thought better of it. On one hand he didn't want to sit in an uncomfortable silence, no matter how short the ride. On the other hand he didn't want to belabor the point. Two minutes later Micro was relieved of his uneasiness when both men caught a glimpse of Bubba, huffing and puffing, his back up against a pine tree looking like he was struggling for his last breath.

Sheriff Jones and Deputy Micro Mitchell burst out in raucous laughter as the truck passed the big man. Jones added insult to injury by saluting Bubba with one of his much coveted pork chop sandwiches. Micro laughed so hard his side hurt, his stomach cramped and his mouth was opened wide but no sound would come out.

Jones almost choked on his sandwich. His vision blurred from the steady stream of tears running down his cheeks and his chest burned from the coughing fit brought on from his food going down the wrong way.

When he was finally able to coax his larynx and diaphragm into submission, Micro was the first to speak.

"Did you hear that pine screaming for relief?"

Sheriff Jones nodded his head in agreement still recovering from his coughing spasms.

"I'm tellin' you Sheriff, you could almost hear that there tree yellin' 'Get ouffa me!'"

"I know'd it. Dat boy is libel to catch a heart attack the way he was breathin'. Maybe we'll send Doc Lane out to the jail on the way back. Check on 'em. See if his ticker still tickin'. He prolly be jus makin' it back by then anyhow."

Micro made a barely audible sound somewhere between a melancholy chuckle and a humph of disbelief.

"Doc Lane is the Colored doc. You know that ole pecka wood ain't gon' let no Colored doc nowheres near him."

"Yeah I spect you right." Sheriff Jones conceded. "But," he paused to make sure Micro was paying attention to the words he was about to say. Micro turned his head towards the Sheriff when his words dropped off abruptly. One eye on the road, the other focused on Jones waiting for him to make his point.

"He's the best. 'Ain't nooo doubt 'bout that."

Micro nodded up and down in response. A truce. The lump he'd felt in his chest evened out. He knew the Sheriff had no ill intent towards his people, so he settled into a quiet acceptance of whatever mission they were going on tonight. He gave a mental thank you to God and switched his mind set to the road they were following.

"Where, exactly, are we going Sheriff?"

"You member that preacher thas been hangin' round? One I got the call bout dis morning from Tommy Boy."

"Yeah, I memba. Gave em three days, right? You don't think morning will see em gone?"

"Ion know. All I do know is I ain't felt right since Tommy Boy called."

"Well, Sheriff, it's always best to......Whoa!" Micro swerved the truck hard to the left. He barely missed the object in the road.

"Watch it Micro! What was dat?"

"Ion know. A deer, a fox?"

"Naw, wasn't nuttin' on fo legs"

Micro looked in the rear view mirror as he gained steady control over the truck.

"Shit!"

""What, you think you hit sumpthin'?"

"No, just realized *who* we almost hit."

"Who?"

"Looked like Lil Janice."

"Ain't that one a Ma Lou's gals?"

"Yeah." Micro sighed. He checked his rearview mirror one more time to see if Janice was still on the side of the road, but his eyes came up empty.

"Think we ought to double back? She look hurt?"

"Naw, she's prolly well on her way home by now it's just up da road. Plus, the last person I feel like dealin' wit tonight is Ma Lou. That woman is crazy."

"Is it true wat dey say, that she...?"

"Sheriff, Iont mean to cut you off, but them loose tongues been singin' that song for a long time. Startin' way back when wit Ma Lou's granny, Fannie Mae. People talk but don't nobody want ta say nuttin'".

"So, is it true or not? And, if it is, why ain't you done nuttin' 'bout it?"

"Sheriff you known me all my life. I grew up round these parts and I know just 'bout everybody in it. Which means, I also know dey dirt. You and I both know ain't no judge gon' hear the case and ain't no politician gon' sign the law when they da main ones dippin' they poles in the dirty water."

Sheriff Jones knew that he'd touched a nerve. Intent on not making his previous words seem like a vain effort he switched tactics.

"Alls I'm sayin' is I ain't one ta turn a blind eye. If you got a way in I got yur back."

"'Preciate it."

Micro thought hard about Ma Lou and her little shack of horrors. That house had been the devil's workshop ever since he was a small boy. If you took the time to listen to the old folks they'd tell you it's been going on as long as the first brick was laid in Topaux.

Fannie Mae was said to be some of the best tail in Topaux. She'd turned Ma Lou's Maw out and when she couldn't handle the scandal she killed herself. Ma Lou was up next and she took to the family business with a vengeance and insanity folks could only whisper about.

He wanted to help those girls. God knows, he wanted to help those girls. Unfortunately, his hands were tied. He'd thought he had a way to stop the madness for good, but out of the blue she stopped talking to him. One day they were making plans for their future and then the next time he saw her she wouldn't even look him in the face. She just turned her head and limped off. She hadn't spoken to him since.

"Thought I had a way, once."

"Was that?"

"I said, thought I had a way once."

Micro took Sheriff Jones' lack of response as an encouragement to continue.

"Cara."

"Ma Lou's oldest gal? The one walk wit da limp? Always look like she 'bout to give out?"

"Dat's her."

"Wasn't y'all sweet on each other at one time? Never know'd what you seen in her, but to each his own."

"She's a good girl! Born into a bad home is all. Now, if you finished judging folks you don't know."

Sheriff Jones held his hands out in surrender.

"I didn't mean no harm, folks talk."

"Yeah, folks like ta talk a whole heap. Problem is they don't neva like ta help."

"Gon' then tell it like you know. I'm listenin'."

"Me and Cara had a good thing going. I knew what Ma Lou was doing but Cara was different. I found a way into her heart. We talked. Real talk 'bout her dreams, and mine, and how we could make 'em mix. I neva took advantage of her, that wasn't what I wanted."

"Sure, I believe you." Sheriff Jones replied sincerely. "Go on."

"Got to a point where she trusted me real good. She would tell Ma Lou she was goin' on dates when she was really wit me. I'd give her a few dollars so Lou wouldn't question it an' everything was goin' fine for a while. Then-"

"Wait a minute Micro. You mean ta tell me you was payin' for another man's good time?"

"You ain't listenin'. I told you I neva took advantage of her. I gave her the money for Lou. I ain't neva touch her. I wasn't payin her for services rendered."

"Alright. Alright. Settle down. I just wanna get da story straight."

Micro paused and gathered his thoughts together. It'd been almost two years. It shouldn't hurt this much anymore. Cara had made a choice. One they'd both have to live with.

"Things went along like so for a few months and then it just happened. Afterwards, I went to give her money like always, for Lou. She told me she didn't want ta remember it like dat. She said..." Micro didn't think he could finish. He'd never shared his story with anyone. After all this time his heart still broke with the thought of it.

He knew what people said she was. He knew that the essence of her innocence had been left in numerous backseats, barns and overgrown fields long ago. But in that moment he felt like she'd found a way to preserve a tiny piece of it and that night she poured it all into him. He'd promised himself that he'd treasure that gift and protect it forever. Micro felt like a failure. His feelings of dejection were complicated by the fact that he couldn't figure out how or why he'd failed.

Sheriff Jones, not normally a patient man, waited for Micro's heart to catch up with his head. No stranger to heartbreak he understood that when a man began to tell a story like this he had to be able to finish it in his own time and in his own way. He needed his Deputy's reflexes sharp, his instincts unencumbered and his spirit free from any guilt or confusion.

"She said... Micro, tonight da beatin' be worth it. I wouldn't let her go; not knowing what she was goin home to. She cried and I begged. She pleaded and I screamed. I had to let her go. Ova da next few weeks we got closer. She shared the hell her and dem other girls was forced to live in. We made plans, plans to take em all away from there. I started seeing some thangs over those weeks. Her hips was changing', rounding out. Her breast felt like dey was heavy in my hand.

We were posed to meet up one night, but she neva showed. I couldn't go to da house. Lou would a killed her. So, I waited. Next time I saw her she was crossing the street dragging that leg behind her. She wouldn't say nuttin to me. Hell she wouldn't even look in my general direction. I didn't push her. I remembered those hips and I waited. It's been two years and ain't no baby ever been talked about round that way."

"She was wit child?"

"My best guess."

| 38 |

Bishop Babcock listened close as Randall ran down the situation to him.

"So, dat nigga Willie dead?"

"As a doorknob."

"You left Jack on em?"

"Had no choice."

"You know he mo concerned wit puttin' that mess in his arm than he is wit kingdom business. Shit, da whole load might be gon' by da time we get back."

"Might be, but he da one wit da shotgun. Had thangs been switched you might not be getting dis message no how. You thank that nigga woulda stayed on task knowin' he needed a taste? Hell naw! He'd a been somewhere leaned up against a tree don't know who tryin ta hold who up."

"We wasting time sittin' here talkin 'bout it anyways," Babcock retorted.

"Hold on, here's the other thang. I seent that fat bastard Junior Deputy come up in here like he was in a hurry. I hid out behind dat big elm out front and when he came out he had the Colored Deputy wit em."

"You think they on ta us?"

"Ion't know, but I ain't willin' ta take the risk, is you?"

Bishop Babcock gave Randall a look that would've frozen any other man. Randall was so tired of his foolishness, the look barely paused him. They moved towards the door to round up the men inside when

Babcock noticed the new bills he'd given the girl flapping in the breeze. Never one to throw away good money he walked towards the gate and picked up the new green paper. A flash of red caught his eye and he added the crumpled handkerchief to his bounty.

The sight of the girl's blood excited Babcock. He knew it was a tight fit, but he didn't think he was the first. He'd heard the girl was part of a stable. If he'd known she was a true untouched servant of God he wouldn't have been so rough, at the least he would've gotten her a bed.

Randall looked on with disgust as Bishop Babcock held the handkerchief he'd given the girl up to his nose and smiled. He swore he could hear the water pooling in his hefty jowls and his heartbeat quicken with desire. This is it, it's not worth it. He has to be stopped.

Babcock pulled himself out of his stupor long enough to begin formulating a plan. He stepped into Tweela's and signaled to his flunkies that it was time to go. Johnson dropped a stack of cash on the tiny table overflowing with dirty plates and followed his boss's lead outside.

| 39 |

Tweela walked over to the table and snatched up the stash of cash thrown in a pile of gravy. Her fingers clenched tight around the handle of the cast iron skillet she held with her free hand. She'd been in the back when Lil Munk finally got up the nerve to come and tell her that the Bishop and Janice were missing from the table.

The busboy wasn't very smart, but he did good work and was usually dependable. Tweela had been running back and forth to the kitchen all night trying to keep the old wood stove hot enough to keep up with the catfish orders coming in from the late night special and the local favorite, pork chop sandwiches. The place was packed and her attention had been split all over the restaurant.

Tweela was rattlesnake mad when the boy finally slunk into the kitchen to stutter his report. She'd seen Janice sitting at the table with the Bishop and his boys and told Lil Munk to watch out for the girl in case anything funny looked like it was about to go down while she was in and out of the back.

She'd told Ma Lou years ago that she'd better not catch her sending those girls in her place to sell nothing that wasn't on her menu. Lou might play crazy but she knew Tweela well enough to know she meant business. Seeing Janice here tonight made her suspicious. She pushed some of her doubts aside knowing the girl was only around twelve and in the company of a Bishop.

By the time Lil Munk came into the kitchen Tweela had breaded, fried and laid ten pieces of fish and six pork chops on yesterday's daily news. Tweela punched him in his chest like a grown man and called him names she was going to have to apologize for later.

She was most mad at herself. If she hadn't been so heartsick, flirting with Micro, she might have noticed that Janice and the Bishop weren't at the big table near the back. When Micro's food was ready she was so intent on getting him his sack and getting in a little side talk, she'd barely glanced at the rowdy men. The Bishop must've slipped out with Janice right before Micro came in, she reasoned.

Tweela grabbed a cast iron skillet from the hook beside the stove and left the kitchen in a rage, determined to smash somebody's head in. Her heart sank when she realized she was too late. Tweela pushed her shoulder into the back door leaving it wide open as she ran to the gate.

There was no sign of Janice.

"God, please let there be some redemption for that girl," she prayed. "Lord, she's just a baby," she cried. "She's just a baby."

Feeling defeated, she trudged back into the diner and strode into the kitchen. She flung the skillet against the wall and made a sizeable dent in the drywall. With a purpose and determination like she'd never felt before, Tweela opened the flat iron disk on the stove and tossed the devil's money into the flames.

| 40 |

Outside Tweela's, Bishop Babcock held an impromptu meeting. The men gathered around him still shooting the breeze thinking this was just another one of the Bishop's pep talks where he blew self-inflating smoke into the rear of anyone who still believed his motivations were honorable and pure.

The men were seasoned grifters. All of them were plucked out of their lives of petty crime to follow a deeper calling; bundles of cash. In the beginning they relished these talks. It gave them a sense of purpose and made them feel like they were giving the people they stole from something in return for their plundering.

Babcock won them over by becoming the father figure they'd never experienced. Most of them fell over themselves and each other trying to please him; to make their Daddy proud. Until, they saw the truth of who their father was.

Once their eyes were opened and their sentiments destroyed, it was the money that held them and bound them to the den of thieves Babcock had welded together. His speeches no longer inspired them. They made fun of his long winded exaggerations. The only man who still believed his own hype was the Bishop himself.

He waited for the boisterous men to calm down. Patient and exacting by nature, he bowed his head and began to pray. Gradually, the men focused their attention on the Bishop until he had their undivided attention. His voice was low and throaty forcing the men to lean in closer to hear him.

"Men, we are on the edge of Satan's lair. Smell the sulfa, hear him hiss, feel his deathly coils on your throat squeezing God's breath from your lungs."

To drive home his dramatic point Bishop Babcock brought both of his hands to his throat. He gasped for air, spinning around in small circles and scanning the ground for the hooves of his imaginary foe. The men hung their heads in disgust, pity, scorn and mock laughter. They'd never let him see the fool they believed him to be.

Emboldened by what he mistakenly took as reverence, Babcock's gesticulations grew in earnest. Keeping one hand on his throat he got down on his haunches and began using his other hand to throw random wild punches at an enemy only he could see.

His fictional competitor seemed to be getting the best of him when Babcock let out a loud guttural war cry. He fought his own hand off his throat. Grabbing the air in both hands he flung it to the dusty ground where he ceremoniously jumped on top of it over and over again to the rhythm of a fast paced double dutch.

"Devil, you have no power here. My feet will bruise your head. My heels grow callous and evade your strike."

People began to make their way to their porches to see who was making such a fuss. Customers filled the windows and doorway of Tweela's. They were curious enough to step away from their plates and dominoes, but not nosy enough to make a full commitment out of the establishment.

Mac, a tall cream colored Creole, was the first to notice the crowds starting to gather. He'd been in a bar fight as a young man. His left eye was permanently damaged and the frayed muscles made the orbit jump out of control in his socket behind his scarred lid. He held his head to the left side and looked up and out with his right, the only position that kept the feeble eye under some control. While the others were immersed in their private thoughts, waiting out Babcock's tirade, Mac was the first to see trouble.

"Amen!" Mac announced abruptly, breaking the men out of their stupor. "Praised be His anointing!"

"Glory ta God!"

"Hallelujah!"

The other men joined in the reverie. They glanced around giving each other looks. Each one urging the other to step in and put an end to the spectacle Bishop Babcock had become. Stepping forward they closed ranks and sealed the circle. No one wanted to be "the one" to interrupt him.

Everyone knew there'd be hell to pay for "burdening" the Spirit of the Lord. None of them knew exactly what the offense meant. But, they all knew it's what Babcock had yelled repeatedly as he beat a man to death in Waxahachie last summer for stepping in on one of his prophecy performances.

Having grown weary of his calisthenics, Babcock was now on his knees, arms outstretched, head reared back face to the heavens, body convulsing uncontrollably as he was overcome with emotion. He squeezed his eyes together coaxing fake tears to stream over his cheeks. He'd managed a small rivulet when Randall decided he'd had enough.

Consequences be damned, Randall stepped into the center of the circle and leaned down close, whispering sharply in Babcock's ear. He stepped back and waited for the fists to start flying, but the Bishop knew what he'd spoken was true. All he could do was give Randall a look that said he wouldn't forget the tally and he'd settle up later.

"Listen up fellas." Randall commanded, bringing the men's attention to him and taking their focus off the tension growing between Babcock and him. "The Bishop's got a word."

Caught off guard, Babcock only had a split second to pull himself together and address his men.

Babcock's face was stone. He fought hard against the voice raging within him to stomp Randall's smug face into the ground for his disrespect. Especially, since it appeared to be spreading among the men. He took his time getting to his feet, hiding his disgust at having to put his hands in the dirt and fury that not one of them had come forward to lend him a hand in his efforts.

In his mind he'd elevated all of these no-count bastards to a life they'd never even been aware existed. He'd reached down into the muck and mire of their lives, cleansed them and made them like new. All of the money, women, booze and food they could stomach as long as they were loyal and obedient to his will. Now, as he knelt before them, no one would extend him this common courtesy?

Babcock stood, wiping palm against palm freeing them of the grit and grime coating them. Methodically, he spun around the circle catching each traitor's eye with a deadly intensity until they dropped them in submission and fear. He didn't bother to look at Randall. For him there would be no redemption. He'd already decided his fate. He waited a beat until he could feel their distress.

"Soldiers! Put on ya armor. The enemy is at the gate. The Lord hath commanded the blessing of the store houses and blessed me in the land. What He gathers for the good of His righteous servant, let no man put to sunder."

The men looked confused but nodded in agreement anyway. They never really knew what he was going on about. Most of the time they listened because his words sounded good and he sounded smart. Already, at his breaking point Randall stepped up again. What the hell, he thought, from his actions earlier he already knew his time with the gang was running near to empty. If he set this up correctly he could leave with the money and his life.

"Look here, Willie dead. Jack got da thief. Shit done hit da fan wit da Sherriff an' if we don't get on up outta here somebody fat sho nuff finna be in the fire."

He had their full attention now. Hatred rolled off Babcock in great heated waves. Randall could feel them lapping at his neck, but he couldn't let them deter him. If he didn't make his move now he'd never be free.

"Primus, Leon, Terry, Mac, Davis and Johnson run on back ta the site an get errythang loaded up nice an tight. Don't leave nuttin behind could lead back ta us."

Randall had to make his next move with surgical precision. Babcock was distracted by his anger but he was no dummy. It wouldn't take him long to figure things out. Until then he had to keep him agitated for as long as possible.

"Me, Rico, Big John and Babcock gon' head ova ta Jack an take care a dis Willie sitchiation. After dat we gon-"

"Nigga, who put you in charge?" Johnson spat, interrupting Randall's instructions.

"Ain't nobody put me in nuffin. And trust me, you's welcome ta carry ya own load best you can." Randall realized it was time to pull out a little razzle dazzle he'd picked up from Babcock before Johnson's question had time to take root in the other men's minds.

Randall addressed the whole group. "Ain't nobody tryin ta take ova. I wanna see my brothas get outta dis here mess wit somethin' sides themselves."

He had to give them a reason to follow. They needed to respect him or they'd look to Babcock for assurance. He scanned the crowd, looking each man in the eye, even Babcock. The heat was still there. His anger was sufficient cover for Randall to strike.

"The way I see it," Randall continued. "Errybody gots a chance ta move out on dey own. If we stick together the deck ain't stacked so high. If we can clean dis up, maybe we can all go home."

The men shook their heads in agreement. Even Johnson seemed to settle down. Babcock stood by and watched. Randall held all the cards right now and Babcock couldn't see past the image of plowing his fists into his face. He forced a smile on his face and shook his head with the rest of the men.

Rico, Mac, Big John and Primus stole glances at Randall and each other. They couldn't believe what they'd heard. Randall said they were going home. For months the five of them had been figuring out how to rid themselves of the albatross around their necks. All they'd been waiting for was Randall's go ahead to signal when the time was right.

Randall discreetly nodded at his co-conspirators in between the looks of affirmation he gave the others. He'd put at least one trustworthy man in each group he was sending out and now it was time to ice the cake.

"When you finish gon' North up ta Princies. We'll hole up there till we all show up an figure out what's gon' happen next."

The men dispersed. Jarmaine and Poteet, the two youngest of the group in age and experience, stood looking at Randall like lost sheep. Poteet as usual was the first to speak.

"What's me and J posed to do?" he questioned sincerely.

"Gon' down to da cathouse and see if any of the men laying up in there. Give em da run down an tell em ta head ta Princies long side er-rbody else."

"Das all?" Poteet asked.

Randall thought for a moment. "Naw. Head up ta da Sherriff's and ax him fo directions."

'Ta where?"

"Ax em how ta get somewhere like Taloosa."

"Oh." Jarmaine was the first one to understand. Poteet looked bewildered. Jarmaine hit him in the arm playfully. "Nigga, it's Taloosa."

Poteet finally understood, Taloosa was south of Topaux. The men took off on their separate assignments. Randall's mind raced as fast he ran with one thought. They were going home, all they had to do was hold on.

| 41 |

Micro pulled the truck up to the edge of the field, previously oc-
cupied by Bishop Babcock and his crew. The clearing was empty and
both men felt uneasy. Closing his eyes and bowing his head Micro had a
quick talk with God. He felt a peace wash over him, allowing the sharp
pain in his chest to turn into a dull thud. Sheriff Jones took some deep
breaths meant to give Micro time.

"You good?"

"Yeah. Past is da past. Besides we got work ta do."

Jones and Micro opened the truck doors simultaneously. Hands
touching their state issued revolvers in preparation. The Sheriff, happy
to be unboxed, stretched his legs to get his blood circulating again. Micro's eyes searched the ground, nerves tight from the eerie silence.

"Looks like they cleared out already."

"Not ta look a gift horse in the mouth or nuttin', seem like dey
cleared out a lil' too clean fa my taste."

Micro thought about what the Sheriff said. He had to admit that
from what they'd heard from Tommy Boy something wasn't adding up.
Babcock and his boys usually stayed around to do a little pillaging.

"Almost like dey runnin' huh?"

"Yeah, Micro, and I aims ta find out from what."

"Sheriff you seen dat? That light flicking off and on like somebody's
moving fast through da wood line?"

"I see it now."

Sheriff Jones fished his flashlight out of his utility belt and pointed
it in the same direction they'd seen the bouncing lights.

"Naw Sheriff." Micro stopped him, using his hand to change the position of Jones' light until it pointed towards the ground. "We don' want em to know we comin."

"How you spect we follow em? Dark as hell out here, moon not even out and da stars barely twinkling."

"I know these woods like da back a my own hand. Prolly done hunted, trapped and killed e'ry animal you could think of in em since I was knee high."

Sheriff Jones had to chuckle. "Better than any bloodhound?"

"You better know it. We losing ground. Let's go for dey get too far ahead. Stay close ta me and step 'exactly where I step.`"

Micro started out when he felt Sheriff Jones' hand on his shoulder. He stopped in mid stride, but didn't turn around.

"Micro how'd you know where we was headin'?"

"Cause, I ain't felt right since I heard the good Bishop Babcock was down near Tallahassee."

| 42 |

"They're coming."

"Yes, Brother, I can feel them."

Maveth paced impatiently waiting for the dense brush to part.

"Racham, if they choose to kill him, we can intervene no more."

"I am aware Brother."

Maveth's pacing subsided. The hairs on his neck prickled.

"Do you feel that Racham?"

"The others? It is possible then. All is not lost."

| 43 |

Anthony watched Jack's eyes roll back into his head and slip into a drug lusting fog. The hitman's gun arm slipped and Anthony was about to pounce on his unsuspecting captor when Randall, Big John, Rico and Bishop Babcock burst into the clearing. Short of breath, the men fanned out around the gruesome scene with Babcock playing the point man.

Anthony froze.

Jack stumbled out of his stupor, blinking rapidly, trying to remember where he was and what he was supposed to be doing. When his focus found Babcock, he swallowed hard. Babcock's expression promised extreme punishment if he didn't get it together. Jack gripped the rifle a little harder and pointed the muzzle a little straighter in an effort to prove to Babcock he'd had the situation under control.

Babcock composed himself quickly. He strode over to Anthony, slowly stalking his prey, never taking his eyes off the boy. Willie's death assaulted his nostrils the closer he got to the boy. He took in a great gulp of feted air and scrunched his nose up into his eyes, showing his revulsion. Eyes still trained on Anthony, Babcock culled the phlegm deep in his chest and spat on the corpse.

Anthony's bowels twisted themselves into intricate knots. Outside, he met Babcock's stare with a ferociousness only the really young or extremely stupid can muster. Babcock found himself both respecting and resenting the boy's cocky demeanor.

Babcock thought about bringing the boy into his fold. There was a place for a young kid like him in his organization, once he'd learned his place. A few hard knocks added to some fierce grooming and the kid might fit right in. Hell, this racket could benefit from some fresh blood.

Glancing at the men around him, Babcock discarded his grand idea for Anthony's new future. He looked Randall in the face and let him see the frost in his eyes. There would be no reprieve, for anyone, tonight.

Fresh waves of anger rippled through Babcock. He remembered Randall's earlier hijack move. For the first time, Bishop noticed how Big John and Rico closed ranks and positioned themselves on either side of Randall.

A lesson would be taught tonight. A lesson to ensure that if thoughts of realignment were in any of the men's minds they'd reconsider their current stance. The boy would die tonight. His only regret was that he wouldn't be able to take his time.

"You had a mind ta cheat me boy?"

Anthony was mute; staring at Babcock defiantly.

"You hear me boy?"

Babcock could feel the men's eyes boring into his back. He imagined them laughing and making fun of him. How could he command the respect of thirty men when he couldn't even make this little backwoods brat speak?

Bishop Babcock was on the edge of blinding fury. Tears sprung into his eyes and rage overpowered him, clouding his vision. He drew his right hand completely over his left shoulder, shifting all of his weight onto his left leg and unleashed a backhand that had Anthony crashing into the wheel of Willie's rusty truck.

"Cat got yo tongue boy? Let me see if I can't help set it loose."

Babcock reached down and grabbed Anthony by his shirt collar. He hoisted his limp body up with one hand and smacked him lightly on the cheek.

"Boy? Boy? Get up."

Anthony's eyes fluttered as he struggled to regain consciousness.

"Eh, boy. There you go. Wake up for Bishop," Babcock cajoled. "Seems ta me a boy who gots eyes on my money ought ta be able ta take a lick. What you thank?"

Tears ran down Anthony's face.

"I say, what you thank boy?"

"Y-y-yes sir," Anthony stammered, not wanting to experience another blow.

Babcock leaned in close to Anthony and whispered in his ear.

"Good. I didn't wanna have ta get after that cat again."

Babcock dropped Anthony on the ground and waited for him to collect himself. Anthony stood up, his head spinning and tried to find a way out of the mess he'd gotten himself into.

As soon as he righted himself Babcock punched him in the face. The ring on his pinky finger knocked his two front teeth loose. Anthony found himself sprawled out on the ground, bits of gravel digging into his back.

"Get up little nigga! Don't think laying there's gonna keep me off ya. If I can't swat ya I'll stomp ya. Either way you gon' get dis ass whoopin'."

Anthony made it up on all fours before Babcock kicked him in the gut. Partially digested beans spewed out of Anthony's mouth as he crumbled onto his belly and gasped for air.

"Get up!"

Reluctantly, Anthony swayed to his feet. Babcock rewarded him with another jab to the face. This time Anthony's nose broke open and blood shot all over Babcock, the truck and Willie.

Rico, Randall and Big John looked on anxiously while Babcock toyed with the boy. They needed him to hurry up and finish whatever he was going to do so they could get the money and get the hell out of Mississippi.

Randall saw the way Babcock looked at him. He knew that look. Everything Babcock did now to the boy, he was sure to do worse to Randall later. They were fighting against time they didn't have.

Rico and Big John knew enough to follow Randall's lead. The plan was to dispose of Babcock somewhere along the way to Princies. Plans would have to change. Babcock was out for blood. The little bastard, barely standing in front of them, was not going to be enough.

Randall stole a glance at Jack. If he hadn't been hooked on heroin, he would have recruited him along with the other men. Jack had been a sniper for the Army in the Korean War. Word had it he'd gone from shooting Soviets and Chinamen to shooting White infantry men. The only reason he hadn't been strung up from a tree or court martialed was because they didn't have any solid proof. They sent him home with an other than honorable discharge and washed their hands of the whole matter.

The thought amused Randall. Jack the junkie was the only colored man he knew who'd gotten a fair trial anywhere on this earth and he chose to go and mess it up by putting trash in his veins. Randall wondered what side of the fence Jack would climb if they went after Babcock now.

Jack was starting to nod. Randall calculated his odds. At any time Jack could come back to the land of the living and make their situation a lot stickier. Randall was still contemplating his decision when a dry branch snapped in the wood line behind the three men.

Everyone froze.

"Who dat?" Jack yelled at the trees.

Sheriff Tommy Jones and Deputy Grayson 'Micro' Mitchell moved from behind the cover of the burch, revolvers drawn.

Jones tipped his hat like a gentleman before answering, "The Law".

| 44 |

Sheriff Jones trained his weapon on Jack.

"Drop it son."

Jack opened his fingers and let the rifle free fall from his hands.

"Hands up. Get on ova there with the rest of em."

"Now all of ya get on the ground, hands on top of ya heads," Micro instructed the four men.

The last place Randall wanted to be was face down in the dirt. He'd tried to stay two steps ahead of the Deputy all night, but Babcock always had to put on a show. This new development could be a blessing or a curse, it was too early to tell.

"You there." Sheriff Jones pointed at Anthony with his revolver. "Step over here a ways."

Anthony could barely see or breathe. He made his way over to the Sheriff, his one good eye wandered from Jones to Babcock, unsure of which man would do him the most harm.

"What's your name son?"

Blood pooled in Anthony's throat, choking him, making it hard to answer. He slumped to his knees, his body shaking uncontrollably.

Sheriff Jones' forehead creased with worry watching Anthony force chunks of clotted blood from his throat.

"Take it easy now son."

"Anthony," he finally squeaked out, his throat raw and burning.

"Anthony, huh? Tell me sumthin, Anthony. Why was you over there gettin' ya face bashed in?"

"Look a here , Sheriff," Babcock interjected.

"Look at what? Boy."

Babcock flinched, drawing his lip up in an involuntary snarl.

Sheriff Jones hated to fall back on the cracker ways he was raised with, but he didn't feel like this so-called man of God deserved any of his respect. He needed him to know exactly what he thought of him. This man had done enough damage in his peaceful town. To see him out here, in his woods, assaulting a child like a grown man had set his blood to boiling.

"I don't believe I was talkin' to you, boy."

"No suh," Babcock had no choice but to bow to the Sheriff's authority. His jawline sharpened from his teeth grinding against each other.

"Tell you what. Since you're all fired up to talk, maybe you can tell me why you was using dis here boy's face as a punching bag?"

"The boy –"

"I ain't done yet. While you at it, explain ta me why this man is laying ova here like a gutted fish?"

"We - "

"Boy, if you interrupt me one mo' time, Imma show you what a heavyweight is all about."

"Yessuh."

"Then, I want you ta tell me how all a dat money got in that there burlap."

In all the commotion no one noticed that Willie's sack had come undone. Faded green bills blew across the make-shift road into the bushes and trees. Anthony, Babcock, Randall, Big John and Rico watched pieces of their dream float away. Jack was the only one unaware of the travelling currency. He was sound asleep, face full of dirt.

Babcock moved to close the bag. Sheriff Jones cocked his revolver and pointed it at Babcock's head.

"I don't suspect you a dumb man, but if you even so much as touch that money, you gon' be a dead one."

The look on Sheriff Jones' face and the timber in his voice let him know that he wasn't joking. Babcock straightened, put his hands up in surrender and took a step away from the money for good measure.

"Let me explain, suh."

Babcock waited for the Sheriff's finger to ease off of his trigger. A few tense moments later it was clear Sheriff Jones did not have the same intentions.

"Speak, boy!"

"The money is mine."

"Yours?" Rico and Big John said in unison.

"Yours? You don't say?"

"What I means ta say is, I, we, are men of the Lord. We travel round preachin' the gospel and saving souls."

"For who?" Micro countered.

"Now Micro," the Sheriff admonished, "let the preacher here have his say. Small advice to you though Bishop," Jones spat to get the bad taste out of his mouth. "you ain't got but so many words ta say it wit' fo' I gets impatient."

"Thank-you suh."

"Just get on wit' it," Micro added testily.

"Like I was sayin' we preaches the word, fa free. Good peoples don't like ta see servants of the Lord without food, shelter, clothes and such."

"I see. And the dead man?"

Babcock bent his head in mock salute of the deceased. Micro rolled his eyes at the bogus show of reverence and made a sucking sound with his teeth in disgust. Sheriff Jones was reaching the limit of how much he was going to take.

"Bishop, I'm gettin' bored."

To his dismay, Babcock lifted his head to find the revolver was still aimed at him. This time it was dead center to his chest.

"My wife's brother, Willie."

"The money man." Micro chuckled. "Sheriff," he continued, "I think I'm beginning' ta see how this thang got laid out."

"Well, hold on Micro. Don't spoil it fa me," the Sheriff cautioned. "Let me see if the good Bishop here will lay it out for me as good as you. I ain't as quick as you, wit all that book learnin' you got. I might need a lil help, from... What you call it Bishop? The Lord's servant."

Bishop Babcock wanted to murder somebody. Outnumbered and outgunned was not a position he found himself in frequently. When they walked away from this Randall and his flunkies were as good as dead. Holding on to that that thought calmed him; allowed him to take some of the hatred out of his voice while he answered the Sheriff's questions.

"So," Sheriff Jones began, "How'd Willie end up wit a knife in the gut?"

"Dat boy over yonder killed 'em." Babcock answered, pointing accusingly at Anthony.

"What boy?" Sheriff Jones pointed at Anthony. "This boy?"

"Yessuh. Killed 'em for the money these good peoples donated ta us."

Sheriff Jones squinted his eyes at Anthony and gave him another hard look.

"What he saying true, son?"

"Yessuh." Anthony answered with uncertainty. His mind, body and spirit had taken a beating and somewhere along the way he'd given up. All he wanted now was for it to be over.

Sheriff Jones shared a look of concern with Micro, who only shrugged his shoulders in response.

"Well then," Sheriff Jones surmised, "looks like it's all settled."

"Thank you suh!" Babcock gushed, full of gratitude. He bowed extra low to Sheriff Jones and nodded his head in appreciation towards Micro as he bent to pick up the burlap sack and what was left of the money.

Sheriff Jones fired his gun and sent a bullet flying past Babcock's head. Babcock cried out in pain, the heat from the expended round burning the tip of his left ear.

"That one was a warning. You must can't hear so well, boy."

His anger peaked, Babcock's nostrils flared and his hands balled into tight fists. He forgot about his subservient posturing and took a menacing step towards his adversary. Sheriff Jones chuckled at his useless display of emotion.

"You mad boy? What you gon' do, fight me?"

Babcock struggled to regain his composure.

"I thought you said it was settled."

"It is. But you ain't got a dog in this fight if you thank I'm just gon' let you walk away wit my evidence."

Micro couldn't stop himself from letting out a deep belly laugh.

"Evidence?" Babcock blurted.

"Yeah evidence." Sheriff Jones replied.

"You sho was right Sheriff. The Lord's servant must can't hear so good." Micro countered, unable to resist taking a jab at Babcock.

"That money was given freely. Ask anybody."

"Still don't change the facts." Sheriff Jones explained. "This here clearing is a crime scene. I gots a dead body and a confession."

"B-b-but,"

"Ain't no buts 'bout it. You said this here youngster stabbed Willie and he said he agreed. The crime happened all cause a this here burlap filled wit money."

Sheriff Jones walked over to the bag of money, gathered it at the neck, picked it up with his free hand and walked backwards, putting a few spaces between him and the Bishop.

"That's what we in the law profession calls evidence. My evidence."

There was nothing Babcock could do to mask the hatred and anger bubbling inside him. His face betrayed his murderous thoughts. Sheriff Jones cocked his revolver again, loading another round in the chamber. He spoke to Micro, never letting his eyes stray from Babcock's feet and hands.

"Deputy?"

"Yeah, Sheriff."

"Everybody good back there?"

"Y'all good?" Micro asked the four men lying on the ground.

Randall, Big John and Rico shook their heads in unison. Jack snored softly.

"They good."

Sheriff Jones backed up until he was shoulder to shoulder with his Deputy. He reached out his hand to take Micro's gun. Both revolvers securely in his hands, he kept one pointed on Babcock and the other on the men at his feet.

"Get da boy and hoist him up, Micro. He aint gon' make it how we going."

Micro did as he was instructed. Anthony lay across Micro's shoulders like a limp rag doll. His stomach pressed against the back of Micro's head; arms and legs dangling on either side of his neck. Sheriff Jones and Micro shared a brief tense look.

"Run!"

Micro took off into the woods, Anthony bouncing heavily around his neck. Sheriff Jones took alternate shots with both pistols in Babcock's direction driving him to the ground before turning and running after Micro.

| 45 |

Big John was the first man up. He ran across the dirt and charged at Babcock. The two men locked in battle, trying to throw each other to the ground. Rico sprinted to Jack's rifle and aimed it at Babcock and Big John, waiting for a clear shot at the Bishop. Randall ran into the woods not ready to give up on the money.

Randall ran back into the clearing out of breath.

"They gone."

"Figures." Rico declared, one eye steady in the rifle's sight. "I can't get a bead on Babcock. Might have to shoot both of 'em."

"Be patient. Last thing we need is-"

Rico and Randall were suddenly tumbling over each other. Jack finally woke up and climbed up the wrong side of Randall's fence. He took out his knife and ran over to where Babcock and Big John were still struggling.

Both men were tired from their contest. Neither one could gather up enough strength to fight anymore. All they could do was hold on to each other, waiting for someone to give up and let go.

Randall scrambled to his knees and grabbed the rifle. He got off a shot, blowing out the junkie's knee before he could reach Big John. The noise from the blast made the two warriors separate; unsure of whose side the shooter was on. Big John, relieved to see the rifle in Randall's possession, walked over to his comrades, giving Randall a clear view of Babcock.

| 46 |

Sheriff Jones and Micro trotted up to the truck. Rico laid Anthony gingerly in the bed of the truck.

"Think we ought to tether him, Micro?"

"Naw, he ain't goin' nowhere, bad as he look."

Two shots rang out in the distance. Sheriff Jones threw Micro his revolver and both men took cover on opposite sides of the truck. They waited to see if any more shots would be heard coming in their direction. Confident the sounds came from a fight they didn't have to be involved in Sheriff Jones and Rico stood, preparing to leave.

Anthony, quiet since he'd told the Sheriff he'd killed the fat man, began to try and sit up.

"Settle down, son," Micro advised.

"Y'all gon' kill me?"

"Ain't nobody gon' touch you, least not while you in my custody." Sheriff Jones assured.

His words did nothing to calm Anthony's pounding heart.

"What's gon' happen ta me?"

Micro and Sheriff Jones stared at each other across the small space of the truck. Sheriff Jones opened the passenger door and threw the money behind the seat. He started to sit down before he remembered the trip out to the woods.

"Hell naw, I aint doing this again. Gimme the keys, I'm drivin'."

"Fine wit me."

The two men happily switched places. Sheriff Jones pushed back on the mono seat and sighed with relief as he stretched out his legs. Micro opened the small door in the truck's rear window to keep an eye on Anthony.

"What's gon' happen ta me?" Anthony repeated.

Sheriff Jones started up the truck and held on as it lurched forward when he took his foot off the clutch. He put the truck in reverse and maneuvered it around, heading back to the county jail.

Speaking softly but sternly, Micro put his face up against the miniature window to answer Anthony's previously ignored query.

"Hush now and get some rest. It ain't up ta us, what happens. Soon as we get back, you belong ta the great state of Mississippi."

| 47 |

"Why are we still wasting time on this one?"

"Mind your tongue Maveth. Is our time squandered when it all belongs to the Master?"

"Forgive my impatience brother. It angers me that he's wasted his numerous chances. Has the Master not withheld his wrath? Has He not looked over his faults and looked upon him with favor still?"

"You, as well as I, know the answers to which you speak. Has the Master not loved wholeheartedly? Has He not shown mercy and grace to them all? He is who He is. Will there not be a time when you are called and I will not be by your side?"

"Will that day bring you sadness brother?"

Racham pondered Maveth's question carefully before he answered. "Is it not our purpose to do what the Master has commanded?"

| 48 |

He couldn't breathe. The house was hot and no matter how many times he adjusted the thermostat he couldn't get the sweat to stop pouring off of him. They were getting close. He could hear the sirens in the distance. The smell of musty bodies, hot piss and old shit enveloped him. The sound of metal on metal echoed in his head. Thomas could feel them closing in.

Fear pitched him back into the cage he'd called home for twenty-seven years. It seemed like a blessing, at the time, when the two law men burst through the clearing to save him. Now, Thomas wasn't so sure. He wished that big gap-toothed nigga had gone ahead and killed him. All he'd ever wanted was to have and be more than what he'd been cursed with.

"Was it too much to ask?" Thomas raged at the ceiling. Hoping God would finally hear his fervent cries. "What the hell do you want from me? Huh? What did you want that I already haven't given you?".

Thomas poured himself two more fingers of whiskey in the silence.

"Just like I thought," he lamented. "you ain't got shit to say, do you?" He challenged, emptying his glass in one gulp. "Fuck it."

Thomas ran his fingers around the left side of his desk. The luxurious wood-would be missed. *Hell, you can't take it with you.* Maniacal laughter bubbled out of him. The soft click of the secret compartment latch, sobered him.

Thomas reached in the deep false bottom drawer and threw decoy papers in a messy pile on the floor. What he needed was in a beat up ammo box in the bottom of the drawer. He clutched the box tight to his chest. *Was this really the end?* Wailing sirens pushed him closer to his answer.

"I won't go back."

The snub nose .45 revolver and box of Remington bullets seemed heavier than when he first placed them there. One by one he meticulously filled each chamber of the gun. There was no other way out. Six bullets, one shot, one kill.

"I won't go back."

Multi-colored lights bounced off the walls of his office, making it look more like an old school basement party than a warrant execution. Thomas shoved the barrel of the gun in his mouth. Patrol doors slamming and policemen yelling across the circular driveway unnerved him.

When the policeman began pounding on his door Thomas came undone. He thought about going out like a gangsta. Guns blazing, taking as many officers with him that were willing to go. He stood up with confidence, but the jelly in his knees changed his mind.

And the battering ram assaulting his door changed the urgency of his final decision. Splintering wood exploded through the foyer. His sanctuary had been breached.

"That door cost more than three of yall's salaries put together!" Tears and spit commingled in his beard. Thomas picked up the nearly empty bottle of whiskey and swallowed the last of his liquid courage. He repositioned the .45 up against the hard palate of his mouth, closed his eyes and pulled the trigger.

A recognizable 'pop' echoed over hard bottom shoes on precious stone. A sea of blue raced up the Italian marble staircase with weapons drawn. They moved from room to room, checking for any active shooter that might still pose a viable threat. Bishop Anthony Thomas's study was the last to be searched.

* * *

"Charlie to base, Charlie to base, over."

"Base, over."

"Suspect found expired at the scene, over."

"Means of expiration, over."

"Suspect appears to have self-terminated, over."

"Details, over."

"Looks like a single gunshot to the base of the skull through the mouth. There's a .45 caliber handgun at the scene, over."

"Any other casualties, over."

"None identified on the initial search. Upon gaining forceful entry to suspect's residence a single gunshot was heard from the first floor. Officers moved in to investigate and found the suspect in what appears to be his study, over."

"Any signs of a break-in or struggle, over."

"Preliminary investigation does not suggest any. The suspect appears to have been alone and drinking at time of death, over."

"Secure the scene and wait for the coroner, over."

"Will do. Charlie out."

| 49 |

"*Good Evening Lakefield. We interrupt your regularly scheduled program to bring you a tragic update on our previously reported Living Waters 'Circle Scam' story. Bishop Anthony Thomas has been found dead by local police on his palatial five acre property. Police raided the elder Bishop's home earlier this evening and heard a single gunshot as they entered the residence. The official police report declares the death a suicide.*

As previously reported Junior Pastor Damian Hardwin is still on the run. Authorities have been unsuccessful in pinning down a location for the young, charismatic preacher. All attempts to apprehend the alleged criminal and co-mastermind behind the embezzlement scam have proven fruitless.

Lakefield PD is requesting that any information anyone may have regarding Pastor Hardwin's whereabouts be called into a special crime tip line. 1-888-CIRCLESCM. Once again the number you can call is 1-888-CIR-CLESCM. Officials are offering a reward for information leading to the apprehension of the alleged suspect.

As always Lakefield, I'm Tracy Phillips bringing you up to the minute news from WKJZ. Your prime source for what's happening in your neighborhood."

| 50 |

Damian sat on his bed, almost all of his bags packed. He looked around at the bare walls and closets of the one bedroom studio apartment. She'd saved him with a few flicks of her wrist. His trip down memory lane delayed his departure. He leaned over to grab his wallet off the dresser and pulled out a faded receipt with an equally faded phone number and an old photograph, pressed in on the corners where he'd carelessly shoved it into his billfold.

Truthfully, he didn't need the paper anymore. He'd long since committed it to memory. The worn receipt was something he kept because she'd given it to him. The picture was of her in better times. How he liked to fantasize about her. She made him pause, second guess his plans.

Damian took a long look in the mirror. His reflection was foreign to him. The gaunt cheeks, ashen skin and hollow eyes looking back at him haunted him. Damian closed his eyes and shook his head in disbelief. The motion reset his vision, but Damian couldn't help but think of the hallucination as a mirror of his soul.

Damian grabbed his keys off the dresser and locked up the apartment before bounding down the steps to his black four-door Toyota Camry parked out front. He started up the car and headed west on Park Avenue. He'd made this ride more than a dozen times over the past several months. East on the freeway, third exit at Market Boulevard, right at the light and a sharp left onto Driscoll Drive.

He pulled into the cul-de-sac and let the car idle for a few minutes before deciding to turn off the car's engine. Damian rested his head on the steering wheel and for the first time in a very long time he allowed himself to cry. Anger, frustration, disappointment, hopelessness and fear pour out of him through a torrent of tears.

His heart is broken in more places than he ever thinks will heal. Damian looked at the house that held a few of those broken pieces. He was about to drive off when the door opened. Janice didn't show her face, but he knew she was beckoning him inside.

Janice started in on him as soon as the door closed. "What is going on Damian? Is any of it true? Did you take those people's money? You're all over the news!"

Damian hung his head in shame and shrugged his shoulders, unable to come up with a suitable answer to his mother's rapid fire interrogation.

Janice grabbed Damian's biceps, shaking him back and forth and screaming into his face. "Talk to me, Damian!"

"What do you want me to say?" he asked quietly.

"I want you to tell me the truth."

Damian walked into the small living room, hoping the distance between them would help him clear his head. He stood in the center of the cozy room with both hands on his head and wondered where to begin. Janice followed closely behind him and propped her bottom on the edge of the overstuffed striped loveseat, crossed her feet at the ankles for balance and waited.

"I don't know what to say to you, to anybody," he said, relaxing his arms and sitting down in the leather easy chair opposite Janice.

"Baby, you have to go to the police. You have to tell the truth. It can't be that bad," Janice pleaded.

Damian stood up quickly and began to pace in circles around the narrow space. "I can't."

Janice took some calming breaths and decided to try another approach. "Damian, I-"

"Mom," Damian said, interrupting her, "I only came to tell you goodbye."

"You're leaving? Where will you go?"

"You know I can't tell you that. They'll find you eventually and when they do I want you to be able to tell them the truth."

Janice positioned her body so that both feet were planted firmly on the hardwood floor. She wrapped her arms around herself tightly and rocked.

Damian swallowed the tears threatening to explode over his eyelids. "Don't do that."

Janice stopped in mid rock and looked at Damian quizzically, "Don't do what?"

"That. The rocking. You only do it when you're upset."

"You think you know me?" she chuckled quietly.

Damian stepped into the kitchen and got the dark roast she kept in the freezer especially for him. He scooped three heaping tablespoons into the filter and filled the pot with cold water before pouring it into the back of the coffee maker.

"Taking some to go?"

Nodding, Damian grabbed the teapot, filled it with water and set it on the gas powered stove to boil. He bent down, concentrating on the space between the eye and the teapot. He turned the knob, waiting to hear the click-click-click of the mechanism in the oven releasing the gas and the whoosh of fire igniting, sucking up the air around it.

Overly concerned with getting the temperature 'just right', he adjusted the knob by miniscule fractions of millimeters until he was satisfied with the flame. When there are no more knobs for him to fiddle with, Damian is forced to look into Janice's eyes. He shifted his weight back and forth on the balls of his feet like a heavy weight champion loosening up for his big fight.

"You plan on boxing somebody in here?" Janice teased.

"No, trying to stay alert."

Janice rolled her eyes, "That the best you got?"

Damian gestured upward with his open palms, "That's all I got."

Her stern expression rebuked his efforts at banter. Janice went back to her rocking, not bothering to mask the worry that consumed her.

"I don't want to have my last memory of you, of us, to end like this."

"The choice is yours," Janice stated bluntly. "You set the rules Damian. You always have when it comes to you and me."

Janice strode towards Damian. She placed her hand on the right side of his face and traced the scar near his eye with the rough pad of her thumb.

"You have a choice."

"It's complicated Janice. It's way too complicated."

"Now, I'm Janice again?"

Damian took his mother's hand from his face and kissed her fingertips before encompassing both of her hands in his. "I messed up Ma, I messed up real bad. I didn't mean for any of this to happen. Believe it or not, when this all started I thought I was doing the right thing."

"Proverbs 14:12."

"What does that-"

"There can be a way which seems right to a person-"

"-but at its end are the ways of death." Damian finished for her. An awkward silence filled the room. Janice and Damian were at a loss for words to win the other over, both wrapped up in the others feelings, unsure of how carefully or recklessly to proceed. They were at an emotional stalemate.

The whistle from the tea kettle interrupted the silence. Damian busied himself with the preparation of coffee and tea; strong and black for him, honey and deep steep for her. He felt out of control and unable to hold back the sorrow swelling inside him. He kept his back to Janice until his feelings were back in check and his face held no trace of heartbreak.

"Here mom, drink this. I made it just the way you like it."

Janice watched him. She took the warm mug Damian offered and let the heat take the chill off of her bones. She thought about her baby boy. A life filled with regrets. A life full of other people's choices and consequences, a life filled with people lashing out through the darkness in ignorance and pain.

She'd given this life to him. Passed it along to him like the raggedy hand me down drawers and dresses her sisters shared. The guilt was staggering, but she couldn't let it consume her, there'd been enough of that.

"It won't work, Damian. You have to know that."

Damian ignored her out of necessity. He didn't want to be disrespectful, he just didn't have a response. He opened the cupboard and got out his favorite travel mug. World's Greatest Son was written in various sizes, colors, fonts and languages. He studied it, turning it over in his hands. "I hate this thing."

"You hate it, but it's the only one you take with you when you visit. *And*, you keep bringing it back."

"What can I say? I'm a glutton for punishment and ugly coffee mugs. It must run in the family."

"So does foolishness. Still doesn't mean you have to grab onto it with both hands and embrace it like your long lost brother."

"And how many of those do I have running around, mommy dearest?"

He'd injured her. Damian's sharp words had found their target. She was an easy mark and he was being unfair. The regret he felt wouldn't be enough to repair them if he kept pushing her away.

"I-"

Janice held up her hand halting his apology. "No. You said what you meant to say. Don't apologize for it now."

"I really didn't."

"You did. Lucky for you, I can see, even if you're blind. Let me be real here Damian. As long as you eat, you'll never be able to run fast enough to escape your own shit."

Damian tried to go back to pouring his coffee, but his normally steady hands shook under the weight of Janice's words. Stronger, steadier hands took over the task. Lovingly she poured, placing all of her hopes and love into the dark concoction before twisting the lid close. Janice passed the mug off to Damian, briefly resisting the exchange, afraid that letting go meant losing him forever.

"Ma, please, I have to go."

Janice released the cup, begging with her eyes for him to reconsider.

"Thanks." He mumbled, before walking out the door.

Janice trailed behind him, helpless, stopping just beyond the front porch. "Never Damian," she whimpered, "never. You can never run fast enough."

Damian jumped into his car and sped down Driscoll Drive back to his apartment to finish packing. He should've never gone to see her. He wished like hell he didn't have to go. He was going to miss her. Janice. His mother.

| 51 |

"Hello?"

The telephone woke Shonen Humphries out of a deep slumber. He'd gone to bed early, missing the evening news. The last few hours had taken a toll on him, mentally and emotionally. As an Elder of the church he'd fielded questions about the upheaval going on at Living Waters all day and he was tired. When he saw M. Fellows light up on his Caller I.D. he did his best to get his head together and speak coherently.

"Shonen?"

"Yeah Pastor, it's me."

A fog of silence snaked through the phone lines affecting the air on both ends. Pastor Fellows knew that he needed to speak to the Elder about church business, but more than that he needed the wise counsel of his friend. Hearing the familiar voice chipped through his last defenses. Mario found it hard to speak without losing the control he'd tried to keep since Shonen had answered the phone.

"Shonen?"

"I'm here."

The floodgates opened and Shonen sat up in bed to listen to his friend's guilt wash away with his tears. When the line went still again Shonen got down to business.

"What are we going to do?"

"I have to confess." Pastor Fellows admitted. "It's my fault, all of it."

Butterflies spread their wings and fluttered through Shonen's abdomen. He didn't want to believe what Mario was suggesting. The man he knew and called friend could never be a part of, let alone be responsible for such an egregious plot against God's people.

"You were responsible for everything?"

"I'm ashamed to say, yes."

"Why aren't the police looking for you?"

"Huh?"

"If you were a part of the fraud, then you should have to-

"Wait a minute. I-"

"pay just as much as-"

"no, that's not what I-"

"much, if not-"

"Shonen."

"more as-"

"Shonen."

"Damian and Anthony."

"Shonen!"

"What? Pastor, I can't let you wash your hands of this with a phone call. You have to call the authorities. Turn yourself in. I'll go with you. Be a character witness."

"Shonen?"

"What?"

"Can you listen to me now?"

"Sure, but it doesn't change the truth."

"Yes, it does." Mario sighed heavily. "I didn't have anything to do with the scam. There's nothing to tell the police because I didn't know."

"Then what do you have to confess?"

"I let this happen. I was given this flock to shepherd and I abandoned them. I let my personal problems get in the way of God's will and desire for His people."

"That mess with Tristine?"

"I should've come to the board when I felt myself slipping but I didn't. I hid behind Damian and used him to wallow in my pity. Tristine took Cameron and left almost a year ago. I was too concerned with what people would say and how they would look at me as a leader when I couldn't even keep my own family together. "

Shonen didn't quite know what to say. He didn't want to hurt his friend, but he felt like he owed him the truth. *After all*, he thought, *secrets are what led us here.*

"Shonen? Did you hear what I said?"

"I heard you."

"And?"

"And? And everybody already knew."

"What do you mean everybody already knew?"

"You got the town crier in your congregation. Do you think Mother Wilson let any amount of juice concerning you stay in her mouth? She's been trying her best to get you ousted. I hate to say it, but this may be all the ammunition she needs."

Mario listened to everything his friend said. He was convicted in his Spirit. Living Waters was supposed to be a place of community where people didn't have to carry their crosses alone. He'd been prideful and disobedient in his actions. He'd set himself apart from the very people he claimed to love and he'd suffered for it, unnecessarily.

"None of that matters now, Shonen. I have a responsibility to God and His people. I can't be led by my position anymore. I have to stand up for what's right. If they vote me out, then I'm out."

Shonen's grin spread far across his face. This was his friend. This was the man he respected and loved as a brother.

"Well, you are still the Senior Pastor, until the Lord says otherwise. I'll contact the congregation and have an emergency meeting set up for tomorrow, around six?

"No. Tonight."

"Tonight? Pastor it's after ten. How many members do you think will actually- "

"Enough. Enough of them will come. I know I haven't earned the right to say, trust me, so I'll say trust God. If you call the meeting tonight they will come. This can't fester overnight. The more time we give the enemy the worse this mess will get."

"What about the board?"

"I'll meet with them before I speak to the congregation."

"Okay, but there's something you should know Mario. Some of the board has been waiting for this moment. They're like a pack of starving wolves surrounding a chicken coop. They know the rooster's been missing and they know the value of the hens."

It saddened Mario to think that there were those who wanted to pillage Living Waters and it broke his heart to admit that he was responsible for leaving the gates open.

"Thing is Shonen, no matter what the rooster's doing, our farmer never sleeps. Set it up."

| 52 |

Damian jogged down the front steps of his apartment building with his duffel bag slung over his shoulder. He threw the last bag into the trunk and closed it with one hand. Something felt off to him. The hairs on the back of his neck stood up and his muscles tensed, putting his body on high alert.

"I'm losing it." Damian knew his mind was probably playing tricks on him. Even so, he still found himself turning in slow circles and searching the shrubbery for an ambush. He felt like someone was watching him, even though he was the only person on the street.

He chastised himself for letting his nerves get the best of him. Rolled his shoulders in an effort to release the feeling of uneasiness that plagued him. None of it helped.

Damian grabbed for the door handle and felt it slip out of his hand. He switched hands and watched in disbelief as his other hand came up empty too. A thin sheen of sweat covered both his palms. The night was a cool 65 degrees, but his hands were covered in sweat. He tried to wipe the moisture off his hands, rubbing his palms over his jeans. Each rub and inspection ending with the same result.

The sweat thickened, giving off an eerie silver-bluish glow. It moved up his arms gradually, covering his torso and neck. Without warning, Damian was thrown up against the car. Arms stuck in the don't shoot position. Panic paralyzes him. A soothing, warmth entwined itself around his back, over his shoulders and between his legs. Damian tried to put his arms down but his mind is unable to communicate properly with his body. The soft heat gently lifted him up like an invisible harness, forcing him to stand on his tip toes, careening over the curb.

"I don't understand, Racham. Why is now the time as opposed to before? Ruach HaKodesh is still there, I can feel Him." Maveth holds out his hands in Damian's direction, questioning his brother in arms.

"He will always reside within those whom He has chosen. Go deeper Maveth. Do you not see the change?"

The soothing warmth instantly turned into a searing heat. Sweat beaded all over Damian's body, dampening his jeans and button-up shirt. The intensified heat concentrated like a ball of fire in the middle of his chest before it cut into the space between his fifth and sixth rib and pierced his heart. Damian opened his mouth to cry out from the pain but the power taking over his body, won't allow him any release.

Heat engulfs his heart like a large hand picking small fruit. Fingers slid through his aortic and pulmonary arteries, ventricles nestled in its palm. The metaphysical hand squeezed the pulsating organ to the beat of the blood coursing through Damian's body.

"Can this be, Racham?" Maveth questions in disbelief. *"Is it to be that this one is so easily won?"*

"Is that what you've concluded?"

"May I confess brother?" Looking discouraged Maveth lets his hands drop.

"Is it for the glory of Elohim? How long do you think He will tarry, brother? Would the plans of The Most High be thwarted by the fear of His messenger?"

"Deeper still?"

"Much." Racham answered with assurance.

Maveth held his hands up towards Damian again. His eyes transformed into black coals tinged in fluorescent blue. His face frowned with deep concentration as his fingers curled inward forming two catcher's mitts.

The hand tightened its grip, constricting Damian's heart until it stopped beating completely. Fire licked at the fluid encasing his heart drying the thin pericardium and singeing the soft flesh. Slowly, the hand loosened its crushing hold and massaged his heart, coaxing it back into rhythm with its host.

The heat retreated sending Damian crashing against the car. His hands clutched at his chest as his screams echoed off the stone walls.

Maveth pulled his hands back suddenly. He felt like he'd been burned. His breath was labored and his eyes lost their righteous glow. Wild ebony orbs strained to focus on Racham's presence.

"Brother? Brother?"

"Yes?"

"Brother, are you there?" Racham touched Maveth lightly on the shoulder looking directly into his eyes, forcing him to connect himself with his friend.

"How do these humans survive?"

"Tell me Maveth, did you see?"

Maveth swallowed hard, closing his eyes, tears flowing freely allowing them to cleanse his spirit.

"This is the flesh? The sin that resides in them is...abhorrent."

"Yet He loves them still, they are His people."

"I did not comprehend."

Racham gave a weary smile. "The reason we are two. Come; is there not much work to be done?"

"We have not failed then?"

"Does the Master fail? Come."

Damian rolled over onto his back making it easier for his lungs to gather sustaining breath. He took sporadic sips of air until the burning in his chest decreased. The acrid smell of burning flesh was still thick in his nostrils when he was finally able to stagger to his feet.

Man, what just happened?

| 53 |

Drizzle misted the windshield of Pastor Fellows Honda Civic. Tiny liquid polka dots popped up on the glass. The sky was crying. From the time he was a little boy he'd always loved the rain. Most people ran inside when the rain came. Not his Nana. She taught him to always celebrate the rain. As soon as she saw or smelled any sign of it, she got excited and sent a young Mario for her rain 'stuff'.

The two of them, thick as thieves, would dig as deep into the red clay dirt as the old passed down wooden spoon would allow. They mixed the dirt with the last jar of rain water they'd collected from the last storm. That was Nana's way. You had to mix the old with the new. To be transformed you had to take something from the past and wash it in the new.

Nana would make a thick paste with the dirt and water and paint their faces with different signs and symbols. While the rain fell they would dance and sing. By the end of their celebration Nana would end up on her knees, crying, thanking God for the rain. He remembered asking her once why she always cried. She told him it was because she had been washed. The rain was God's love. After it cleaned her on the outside, it filled her on the inside. So much so that it overflowed from her tears and turned into joy.

She'd take him up into her arms and fold herself around him. He would nuzzle his face into the folds of her neck and just breathe. No matter what she'd been doing she always smelled like sweet potatoes and cinnamon.

Whenever the rain came Mario swore he could smell freshly dug dirt, green grass and sweet potato pie. He prayed God was as close to him, in this moment, as his Nana was. He craned his neck to look up at the ornate cross balanced on the steeple of Living Waters. "Lord, help me to carry my own cross."

The parking lot was filled to bursting. Even the CME's had shown up for the spectacle. Driving onto the lot was like driving onto the edge of the abyss. This place was once his second home, but the old familiarity had been lost. All because of his ego and his debilitating neglect.

Mario navigated his sedan into an undesirable ill-lit corner. The symbolic vanquishing felt like a prequel to what was in store for him. His pity party was well under way when three sharp taps on his window prevented him from cutting the cake. He was reaching down between the seats to make contact with the butt of his .9 millimeter, just as a chance glance at his would-be attacker made him blow out air he hadn't realized he'd been holding in.

"You scared the mess out of me, Shonen." Mario said, as he rolled down the window.

"Sorry, man. I didn't mean to startle you."

"What're you doing out here anyway? The sky looks like it's about to open up any minute now."

"I've been out here looking for you for the last fifteen minutes." Shonen's face showed the strain of organizing the past few hours and deep concern for his friend.

"What's wrong? What happened?"

"Nothing. Yet."

Mario sat up in his seat subconsciously preparing himself for the news that had his good friend so stressed. "Give it to me straight Shonen. I'm a grown man."

"Well, I guess in all the excitement earlier I forgot to mention to you that Mother Wilson got her son elected to the Board while you were gone."

"No, not Joe," he exclaimed, shaking his head in disbelief. "Who appointed him?"

"Thomas."

"Who gave Thomas the authority to appoint anybody for anything?"

"You did," Shonen replied bluntly.

Pure amazement glossed over his face. "I did?"

"You did."

"I know I've been out of it for a while, but I never would have given my consent, written or verbal, to give Thomas that kind of power."

"You approved it when you disappeared. I don't mean to tell you I told you so but, I told you so. The minute Mother Wilson brought that storefront preacher into our midst; I told you he was up to no good. I told you not to let that phony Bishop title float out to the congregation without checking his credentials."

"For somebody who doesn't want to say something, you sure don't have a problem saying something." Mario joked.

"It aint funny!"

"I know, man. Nothing about this is funny. I just need you in my corner in there, man. I need a praying somebody in my corner who's not letting his prayers be colored by his anger with me."

Placing both hands on either side of the car door, Shonen eyed Mario trying to gauge his feelings. "I ain't mad. I'm hurt, disappointed and irritated to the nth degree, but I ain't mad. And I need you to know what you're facing in there."

Mario held a single finger up to Shonen, signaling for him to wait. He rolled the window up, turned off the ignition and swung his car door open. Shonen backed up a few steps to give him room to maneuver himself out of the car and folded his arms across his chest. Mario took a handkerchief out of his back pocket and wiped water from the side of the car. Leaning up against the dry spot he created he took a similar stance as his best friend.

Mario looked up at the sky and shrugged his shoulders in defeat. "Rain stopped."

"Pastor?" Shonen implored.

"I'm at a lost Shonen. Tristine leaving was easier than this. I've been on my face praying and I'm still at a loss."

"Standing out here with me being flippant and funny aint liable to help none either."

Mario winced. "Guess I deserved that."

Shonen unfolded his arms and loosened up his posture. "Look man, I know you're heart and I know your mind. We've been friends for a long time. You've helped me through some rough times. In my darkest hours you picked me up from some even rougher places, without hesitation, and didn't tell nobody where you got me from. When I called you drunk off my tailbone, after Sheila died, you got up out of your bed in the wee hours of the morning and you came and got me."

"I remember."

"My point is you've always been there for me, but the one time you most needed someone to be there for you, you shut down. Friendships, relationships are a two way street. You robbed me of the opportunity to be the friend to you that you were to me. And you ain't learned nothing because you're about to do it again."

The sharp words bore into his conscience. He'd stopped accepting his friend's phone calls for prayer months ago. Shonen hadn't seemed to care, his persistence never wavered. When he couldn't reach Mario he left his prayers on the voicemail. Feelings of humiliation morphed into bitterness and Mario started deleting the messages as soon as he heard Shonen's voice.

It hurt his pride to acknowledge Shonen was right. He'd prayed for God to give him strength and help him, but he was still trying to figure things out for himself. *Father, I submit completely to your will. Forgive me for not accepting the answers that you have so graciously given.*

"I'm sorry. I should have trusted you, should have trusted God. Thank you, for sticking with me man. Even when I did my best to push you away, you-"

"Apology accepted. Let's get down to business."

"So, what do we do, now?"

"The first thing we're going to do is stop standing around out here like school girls in bobby socks and pigtails talking about our feelings. Man law #348."

"Fair enough," Mario couldn't help laughing out loud at Shonen's assessment of their dual violation of Man Code 101. "Tell me about this Joe situation."

"Well, a few months after you left Thomas and Mother Wilson got the church all hyped up about there not being any clear leadership. Don't get me wrong, Damian did the best he could, he's a good young man, but those two," Shonen spat in disgust, "were thicker than Popeye's biscuits."

"You know, that whole thing with Damian really bothers me. I don't know what happened, but I'm telling you he was tricked as much as everyone else. It doesn't sit right with me. I'm not saying he's completely innocent, but there are pieces of the puzzle that don't fit. I know Damian, you understand what I'm saying to you?"

"Yeah, shucks, I thought I knew him too."

"No, Shonen. I'm telling you I know that young man's heart as well as I know my own and as well as you know mine. I fed him, like he was my own. You have five son's right?"

"You know I do. You baptized all but one of 'em."

Mario couldn't help but smile. "There's always one. How's Abdul Farid Humphries these days anyway?"

Shonen cut his eyes at Mario.

"My point," Mario continued, "is that you know your kids. They're not angels-"

"By no means," Shonen interjected.

"-but you know at the core who they are. Nobody could come to you and say for instance, Farrow cheated them out of anything on purpose."

"Naw, that'd be Kenyatta, he's the sneaky one."

"Exactly. If I could talk to him, reach out to him somehow..."

"I agree, but until he comes out of hiding, all we can do is deal with the here and now."

"No one's seen him?"

"Not a soul."

"I tried calling him a few times, but his phone goes straight to voice-mail." He sent out a silent prayer on his behalf before forcing his attention back to Shonen.

"I don't mean to sound cold blooded, but we've got bigger fish to fry. That fool Thomas got in the pulpit and tore up 1 Peter 2:25."

"He preached?"

"That he did. He whipped people up into such a frenzy about being lost sheep in need of a Bishop to lead them back to the mighty Shepherd, you would've thought we were Pentecostal."

"That's not what that scripture says."

"I know that. You know that. Before Thomas had the gall to stand up before God and everybody twisting the truth, if I was a betting man, I would've thought that at least three quarters of Living Waters knew that too."

"Where was Damian? Surely, he wouldn't have let him say those things without some sort of reproach."

"Conveniently, he wasn't there."

"Conveniently?"

"Yeah, from what I remember some woman broke into his place. I'm telling you Pastor it was like a spell had been cast. Don't look at me funny, I ain't one to make leaps without reason to jump. I'm telling you it was like something took over the whole church. There were only a few of us standing around looking like what the heck is going on? By the time we came to our senses, it was over."

"So, what kind of power-"

"Never Would Have Made It" blasted from Shonen's hip, and interrupted their conversation.

"Hold up."

Shonen fished his cell phone out of its holster and turned his back to Mario walking forward a few paces to give himself some privacy.

"Hello?"

Mario rubbed his forehead with the palm of his hand trying to picture what Shonen was describing. Bishop Thomas was not a roadblock he'd anticipated. He thought the old man was quirky and a little odd. He never understood Shonen's distaste or mistrust of the man.

Shonen ended his phone call and walked back over to Mario's car. He wiped his hand over his mouth and exhaled.

"What?"

"You'll never believe it."

"What?"

"I can't believe it."

"Shonen, come on man. What won't we believe?"

Shonen shook his head in disbelief.

"Thomas aint gonna make it tonight."

| 54 |

Terror paralyzed Damian long after the mysterious force released him. He wasn't sure if getting up would anger it, so he stayed down and waited for a sign that the coast was clear. A police cruiser turned down Damian's street, lights flashing and sirens blaring. Damian wasn't sure if that was the sign he was looking for, but it was enough to get him moving.

He hoped the officer hadn't noticed him rolling in the grass. Or if he had, he'd figure he was another crazy Black man and none of his concern. Who was he kidding? There was an All Points Bulletin out for him. This would be the one time he'd definitely fit the description.

He prayed that when he tried to open his car door there wouldn't be a replay of his first attempt. Damian got up, but stayed low. His hands were dry and Damian took that as another good sign. *Third sign is a charm,* he thought, when he heard the familiar click of the lock mechanism give way.

All the signs and omens in the world wouldn't settle his nerves. Damian was physically back in the driver's seat, but he was far from being in control. He'd barely checked his mirrors before he zoomed out into the street. The long, loud honking of a red Fiat Sport flying down the street pressed him back to the curb.

"Stupid, stupid, stupid," Damian berated himself and punished the steering wheel with his fists for his idiocy. "I must be trying to get caught."

Damian had no idea where he was going. His first instinct was to head south on Interstate 95. Maybe he'd go down to the Florida Keys and get himself a job on a fishing boat. Long hours and hard labor was what he needed to lose himself. One thing was for sure, he was a sitting duck if he didn't move. His foray into traffic was made with a better eye to safety than before.

What he wanted, more than anything, was to disappear. To go somewhere and be anonymous. He'd had enough of the notoriety, of people pulling on him and expecting him to have all the answers all the time. He tried to convince himself that he wasn't a "Cheers" kind of guy.

He had to be honest with himself. It wasn't the people, it was him. He'd forgotten who he was. He hadn't felt this disoriented since his last year in college. It was the year he lost Cara, with her went his champion.

Cara's cancer was still new his last year in high school. She hadn't been worn down by the nauseating chemotherapy or the endless holistic treatments. He tried to convince her that he wouldn't mind staying closer to home. That he'd gladly give up his full ride football scholarship to Templeton University in order to take care of her.

He'd always known his Aunt Cara to be a very mild mannered Christian woman. By the time she finished trampling on his pride he was scared not to go to Virginia in the fall. She drove him to the airport in July for preseason practice. They joked and laughed all the way to Atlanta.

He teased her relentlessly, poking at the pudge she'd grown over the years. She hated it and loved it at the same time. Told him not to worry about her, he better not go up there and mess up that scholarship by gaining the freshman fifteen.

When she dropped him off at his terminal he waited for her to ask him the same thing she always asked him when they separated from each other. Every day, sometimes several times a day, depending on his activities, it was the same thing. It didn't matter if he was going to school, going outside or going to practice. She always asked the same thing. He thought she'd forgotten when he waved goodbye to her, his luggage piled up precariously in his eagerness to get his baggage checked.

It dawned on him that she hadn't cried in the car or at the curb. *Maybe she's glad I'm leaving. Hard to say you miss somebody when you won't.* He'd told her all week, and at least five times that he could count on the two hour ride to Hartsfield International Airport, not to make a scene. Aunt Cara stayed strong, exactly like he told her. While he, on the other hand, was close to tears all because she'd forgotten to ask him.

"Damian?" She called out to him as the automatic doors opened on his new life. Her voice quivering as it carried. "Who are you Damian?"

"I'm a child of the King."

"You bet not get to Virgin-ga and forget it either," she warned before getting in her car and driving off.

She wasn't the same when he came home for Christmas break. He walked out of the Delta terminal and wasn't shocked when he didn't see her. She was notorious for picking him up late. He wondered what story she would have for him this time. He laughed, knowing that her hopping out the car saying, "See what had happened was..." would substitute for a hello.

He sat down on a bench to go over his Biology 101 notes when an old woman pressed up against a car caught his eye. She was small and weak looking. Like it was all she could do to muster up the strength to lean on the car and not get carried away by the wind.

Damian walked up to her and politely asked, "Ma'am, you ok? Do you have some family here? Do you need me to call somebody for you?"

He was a little put off when she sucked her teeth and rolled her eyes at him. She took the wind totally out of his sails when she said, "Boy stop playing with me and get your narrow hips in this car."

"Aunt Cara?"

"You mean to tell me you done went all the way up to Virgin-ga to come back deaf, dumb and blind?" She threw him the keys and opened the passenger door. "You drive. Your Auntie is tired now."

For two hours Damian drove in shock. Cara's breathing was so shallow he couldn't tell whether she was alive or dead. Her chest barely rose. If he looked over at the wrong moment, it didn't look like she was moving at all. He kept putting his hand underneath her nose to see if he could feel the warm air pushing out from her lungs.

They were getting off on the exit for home when Damian looked over at Cara and almost crashed the car when she didn't appear to move for what seemed like a full minute to him. He took his two fingers and held them close to her nose and didn't feel anything.

Damian was in a full blown panic when he heard her say, "Boy, I been smelling your stanky tail fingers for two hours. We almost home, can I breathe regular air now?"

Cara careened between life and death for three more years. No matter how much he begged and cried, none of his pleas or tears could save her. Two weeks into his Senior year at Templeton, Cara lost her battle with cancer.

| 55 |

Shonen and Mario stood outside Living Waters conference room. Shonen rubbed the remnants from the oil on his finger into his hands. He bowed his head in agreement with Mario and placed one hand on his shoulder so they could pray.

"In Jesus name Amen," Shonen finished.

"Amen."

"You ready?"

"As I'll ever be."

All conversation stopped when Mario and Shonen entered the room. The other seven members of the Board; Elder Walter E. Curley, Deacons Arjan Badal, Jo Wilson, Michael Woodruff, Peter Mann and Deaconess' Diana Crawford and Robin Mitchell, sat around a large oval table wearing stern expressions. Shonen remained standing behind Pastor Fellows. He was intent on showing his unwavering support for his friend. No one moved from their seats to greet them.

Mario studied the expressions on the faces looking up at him. Most of the Board members tried their best to keep their feelings to themselves, closely hidden behind stone demeanors and tight smiles. But, the hate staring at Mario through the eyes of Jo Wilson, Arjan Badal and Diana Crawford was clear and driven.

Each of them had their own ax to grind with Pastor Fellows. Jo was blinded by his obsession with pleasing his mother. At 45 years old he'd been divorced three times. Three ex-wives, all of them bumping heads with Mother Wilson and all of them leaving when they realized Jo would never take anyone but his mother's side. For Jo, Pastor Fel-

193

lows' continued refusal to appoint him to a leadership position was to blame for Mother Wilson's lack of approval.

Arjan Badal had always thought Pastor Fellows was too loose and free with the way he ran the church. He was a man who valued tradition over truth; condemnation over compassion. In Arjan's world rules were meant to be followed and anyone who broke them deserved the full wrath of God and the complete scorn of Arjan. He was more than old school, he was Old Testament.

Of the three of them Diana Crawford's ax was the sharpest. She was a good steward of the church, taking her responsibilities to its members seriously. In her heart she felt she had a duty to fulfill at Living Waters. That duty was almost waylaid ten years ago when Pastor Fellows made a decision Diana could never forgive him for. He allowed women to preach.

Elder Curley was the first to speak, nodding as he acknowledged the two newcomers, "Elder Shonen, Pastor Fellows. Are you ready to begin?"

"Yes." Pastor Fellows answered and for the first time tonight Shonen heard the true weariness in his best friend's voice.

"Do you have anything you'd like to address to the Board before we begin," Curley asked.

"What is there for him to say?" Arjan questioned in his clipped British-Indian accent. "He has neglected his duties and abandoned his post. He is a shepherd who has forsaken his flock."

"That's right," Diana chimed in, "I'm not sure why we're even pretending that this meeting is for anything other than show. The allegations are clear and the evidence is overwhelming."

Shonen saw the slump in Mario's shoulders. He started to move in closer, to stand side by side with him, but decided against it. Their words were hurtful, but he knew the truth in them needed to be heard.

"And enough is enough." Joe added unnecessarily.

"I couldn't agree more." Shonen replied dryly and cut his eyes at Joe Wilson. "And contrary to what any of you believe, this meeting ain't for show. I will be the first member of this Board to admit that a great injustice has been done. However, while we're talking about duties, allegations and evidence," Shonen took his time to look into the eyes of every Board member while he spoke, until his vision rested on Elder Curley, "remember that this is supposed to be a fair hearing and not a lynch mob."

"So noted Elder." Curley nodded and continued, gesturing to the empty chair across from him. "Please have a seat. Pastor if you'll remain standing. All eyes closed and every head bowed, let us pray."

| 56 |

Aunt Cara would know what to do. Aunt Cara always knew what to do. If she were here she'd know exactly what to do. Damian let the depth of his loss bubble up to the surface and boil over. Fresh tears fell until a burst of anger pushed them back. Damian was sick of feeling sorry for himself and he was pissed off that he'd allowed himself to wallow.

"What in the hell am I doing?" Damian asked himself after pulling his car onto the right shoulder of the vacant highway. He killed the engine and looked out into the darkness. He was restless and the sudden need for more air, pushed him outside of the car to contemplate his next move.

He could always go back and try to explain what happened. "Who would believe me? No one, absolutely no one." He'd signed the papers and it was his name on the accounts. All of the evidence pointed to him. There was no way he could explain any of it away.

He couldn't even begin to imagine having to face his mentor. What would Mario think about what he'd allowed to happen at Living Waters? Even if he were able to go back and plead his case successfully, there was no way he could build back the love and trust Pastor Fellows had given so freely.

That was the fear Damian couldn't face. The thought that froze him and any plans he'd had of returning. There had never been a stable man in Damian's life. He didn't know what having a father felt like, but when Mario chose to take him under his wing he knew that what he'd missed didn't compare to what he'd been given.

| 57 |

"Alright y'all, it's late, let's get down to business." Elder Curley instructed, stifling a yawn.

"Can I say something first?"

Mario took their silence as an allowance if not a true affirmative. He cleared his throat nervously, several times, before he spoke. With each guttural intonation, he shoved his emotions down until they were past his stomach, until his shoulders straightened and he was able to speak without his voice betraying him.

"The first thing I wanted to say is that, I'm sorry. I know that I could never say it enough, for what it's worth, I am truly sorry."

"For what it's worth? For what it's worth?" Diana Crawford exploded. "What it's worth is nothing. What it's-"

Elder Curley held up his hand, halting Diana's tirade. "Deaconess," before he turned his attention back to Pastor Fellows, "anything else Pastor?"

"No, Elder, that's all."

"Disgraceful. This whole ordeal is completely disgraceful."

"Deacon Badal," Elder Curley called, catching the middle aged man's attention with the slight warning in his elevated tone, "this will be the last time I say this, to any one; we will conduct ourselves, all of ourselves, with the dignity and respect befitting this Board. Do I make myself clear?"

Most of the Board members readily nodded their consent to the adherence of Elder Curley's guidelines; even Joe shook his head up and down in obedience. Icy stares are all that Arjan and Diana give as their response.

"Elder Shonen, will you read the charges made against Pastor Fellows?"

| 58 |

Damian sped down Highway 95, consumed by his thoughts. Fear gripped him by his throat. The sound of sirens came out of nowhere. He gripped the steering wheel with knuckle breaking intensity. Seeing the lights through his rearview mirror made all of his muscles contract automatically. Cold sweat fell down his back, dampening his waistband. Damian felt like his whole body was turning into a block of ice.

When the black and white cruiser passed, Damian's muscles uncoiled as fast as they clenched. His body ached from trying to hold himself together. Nerve endings in his hands and feet came alive one by one, the pain of a thousand needles shot up his arms and legs.

The close call reminded Damian of how fragile his current ties to freedom were. A life on the run was beginning to lose its shiny new appeal. He wanted to look into the rearview mirror and see if the first cruiser was a prelude to a second or third. Half of him was deathly afraid his relief was a set up. The other half of him needed to solidify his self preservation; needed to know that whatever time he had left, however things ended up, would be his choice. Paranoia drove him to take a quick peak.

Dark orbs met his reflection.

| 59 |

"Pastor, you've heard the charges brought against you before this Board. What say you in answer to what's been said?" Elder Curley questioned.

Pastor Fellows took a long pause before addressing the members of the Board. "I answer the charges as being true."

"That's it!" Diana leaped out of her chair. "That's all I need to hear. I motion for the immediate removal of Pastor Mario Fellows as the Senior Pastor of Living Waters and as a member of this Board."

"Diana?"

"Don't Diana me, Elder! What else do you need to hear? The man has admitted his guilt."

"What I need to hear, what we all need to hear is the man's heart."

"I am not understanding the problem here." Arjan stood shoulder to shoulder with Diana, truly confused by the older Elders statement.

Deacon Michael Woodruff, silent since Pastor Fellows and Elder Shonen entered the small conference room, decided to finally speak up. "Arjan, why don't you and Diana have a seat and listen to what Elder Curley has to say."

"Oh, now you are wanting to speak up? I see you and Brother Shonen have been speaking and conspiring together."

"That's Elder Humphrey to you Deacon and I'll thank you to leave me out of your accusations."

Arjan knew that insighting Shonen was unwise of him and directed his response towards Michael instead. "Is he speaking for you now, as well Michael?"

"Now wait a minute, Arjan. I have sat through many a night and listened to you and Diana postulate about what this Board should do about Pastor Fellows and-"

"And I thought we were all on the same page, Michael?"

Michael lowered his eyes shamefully and let the weight of Diana's cloaked accusation bounce around the room, rendering everyone silent as they waited for Deacon Woodruff's response. An answer in either the affirmative or negative would confirm the innermost thoughts of every member of the Board.

"We were," Michael admitted. "But now we're here." The revelation gave him the gumption he needed to meet Pastor Fellows questioning gaze. "I'm willing to listen."

"Do not flake out on us now." Diana seethed.

"I'm not flaking on anyone."

"I do not mind saying you are looking like many coconuts to me, Brother," Arjan interjected.

All eyes turned to Deacon Jo Wilson as he tried, unsuccessfully, to hold back his spontaneous laughter. His sudden outburst and childish attempt to cover his inappropriateness, caused Diana's growing fury to fall directly onto Jo's shoulders.

"Is there something about this situation that amuses you?"

Diana waited until her lethal stare shrunk Jo's spine significantly enough to bow his shoulders and curve his neck before she addressed the room.

"I am starting to doubt that any of you understand the gravity of what we are dealing with here tonight." Diana pointed directly at Pastor Fellows. "This man deceived us. He took the trust we placed in him and, and, and used it to destroy this congregation!"

"Cut the dramatics Diana!"

"If you think me standing up for the souls we've been elected to disciple and shepherd is being dramatic, then I can see why you and Mario are so buddy-buddy." Diana spat her last words at Shonen and Pastor Fellows.

"That is enough Diana."

Diana feared losing ground and refused to heed Elder Curley's warning.

"These are the men you've decided to hitch your wagon to Michael? These are the men you want to stand up for, after all they've done?"

Michael focused on Diana, and chose his words carefully before he spoke. "I'm willing to listen."

"James 1:14. But each person is tempted when he is lured and enticed by his own desire." Diana spits at Michael.

"What is that supposed to mean?"

"It means Brother, do not let your own desires tempt you into not seeing the truth about what is going on here." Arjan interjected.

"That is not what that means," Shonen argued, "and we are not going to sit here all night and misquote scripture out of context just cause you and Diana are in your feelings."

"You are being the expert on scripture Brother? How about 'the wages of sin is death'? Do you prefer that one?"

"Not if you're going to skip over the rest of it that says 'the free gift of God is eternal life in Christ Jesus'. I do remember I John 1:9 that says, 'if we confess our sins, he is faithful and just to forgive us our sins and to cleanse us from all unrighteousness'."

"Everyone have a seat." Elder Curley commanded, interrupting the impromptu Bible battle. "You too Shonen. We all know that you support Pastor Fellows. You standing beside him like a centurion warrior is not helping. And you two," Elder Curley nodded his head in the direction of Diana and Arjan, "not another word from either of you, unless I ask you to speak. Deacon Woodruff, thank you for your candor. Pastor Fellows, you have the floor."

"Thank you Elder."

| 60 |

Damian fought to keep control of his car. Those eyes. He'd seen those eyes before. His mind searched for a reference point. Those eyes were the last thing he saw before the Camry parked itself up a colossal turkey oak and the airbag punched him in the face.

"Was there not a better way?"

Racham and Maveth positioned themselves beside the wreckage listening for Damian's breath and sensing his heartbeat.

"What would you have me to do? Did you not direct me to get his attention?"

"Oh, so your hearing has not been impaired? I said, get his attention, not drive him up a tree. What good does it do us to come this far and fail in our mission because of your love of theatrics?"

"Are you accusing me of showing off Racham?"

"Are you denying it?"

Maveth feigned seriousness. "Yes. If I were guilty of the thing you are accusing me of I would not have held back the smoke."

Racham turned his back on his friend to hide the smile emerging across his face. Damian's moans floated out of the vehicle and signaled a beginning to the end.

"It is time."

"May Abba continue to bless and provide," Maveth responded before he followed Racham deep into the woods.

| 61 |

"Let's take a vote. All in favor of the dismissal of Pastor Mario Fellows as Living Waters Senior Pastor and member of its Executive Board say 'aye'."

Elder Curley is barely able to get the proclamation out before Diana, Arjan and Jo shout in unison, "AYE."

"So noted. Let the record show that we have three 'ayes' from Deacon Arjan Badal, Deacon Jo Wilson and Deaconess Diana Crawford. All in favor of keeping Pastor Fellows as the Senior Pastor of Living Waters and as a member of this Executive Board say 'aye'."

Pastor Fellows looked to his friend of many years when there were no 'ayes' on his behalf. Shonen returned the look with a nod of reassurance.

"So noted. Let the record show that no 'ayes' have come forward. All in favor of reinstating Pastor Fellows to Senior Pastor of Living Waters and as a member of this Board after a period of restoration of as little as 6 months but for no more than 1 year say 'aye'."

"'Aye'," Shonen said immediately.

Michael Woodruff's vote didn't come with the same alacrity as Shonens. "'Aye'," he finally said after long minutes of thought.

"And you Elder? What say you, Curley?" Shonen queried.

"I say 'aye'."

"A tie? A freaking tie. You mean to tell me I got out of my bed in this weather for a tie? Michael Woodruff, you disappoint me."

"Not as much as I've disappointed myself, Diana, not nearly as much as I've disappointed myself."

Diana grabbed her purse and headed to the door. "This Board is a farce. You couldn't pay me enough to stay here and waste any more of my time trying to figure this mess out. You all can sit here kissing the hindparts of the man who abandoned you, but I've had enough."

"Diana." Elder Curley called out softly, "if you quit this Board your vote no longer counts. Are you sure that's what you want to do?"

Without a word, Diana returned to her seat.

"Elder, if I may? I don't think the Board is equipped to make this decision by themselves."

"Well ain't you a cocky one? You, sir, have no rights to tell this Board anything. You are barely out of the frying pan and now you're trying to direct the rest of us into the fire."

"And I'm not planning on burning in this life or the next, for nobody!" Jo added.

"Really, Jo? For nobody?" Shonen asked sarcastically. "Everybody at this table knows if your momma told you to burn, you'd break your own legs trying to get the kerosene and light the match."

"Can...we...let...the...Pastor...finish...please?" Elder Curley requested in a voice that was both heavily burdened and emotionally fatigued. He rubbed his temples in small circles before continuing. "And I promise to our Father in Heaven if all of you children don't stop this idiotic bickering and let us continue with the business at hand, you will see a side of good old Elder Curley that would make the Four Horsemen bow down in submission." Confident in his rebuke he signaled for Pastor Fellows to finish without waiting for a response from any of the Board.

"While I respect the decision of this Board and the feelings of the individuals in it, I think that Diana made a very valid point earlier. I hurt the people I was given to shepherd. I selfishly endangered their hearts and put my pride above their needs. Everything that I've ever said from that pulpit deserves to be questioned because when I was in trouble, when I was I was in pain; I did the opposite of what I've been preaching for years. I destroyed the safe place we've all worked so hard to build. If I'm allowed to go through this restoration process here at Living Waters, whether it ends in me being reinstated as the Senior Pastor and a member of this Board, or not, I think the decision should be up to the congregation."

Elder Curley used his cane to balance himself upwards and commanded, "Let's go."

"Go where?"

"To the people, Jo. We're going to the people."

| 62 |

Damian willed himself not to scream. He mentally commanded his muscles to stretch and contract to prove to himself that he was still whole. His full body assessment didn't detect any part of him in pieces or damaged beyond movement. He finally opened his eyes and the sight of the hood giving the tree trunk a hug was too much for his fragile state of mind. Fresh tears of gratitude and regret spewed up from a well deep inside of him.

When it was dry, his mind reflexively switched to survival mode. He let out a breathy *Amen* when the seatbelt unhooked and slid off easily. His hope for escaping the metal death trap lifted until he tried to open the door. Using his left shoulder for power, Damian crouched low, reminiscent of a defensive back pose and slammed into the door repeatedly. A loud 'crack' reverberated in the darkness seconds before Damian's roar threatened to blow out the windows.

"Ugh, my life!" Damian dropped his head back on the head rest, and held his dislocated shoulder up with his free hand. "I give up. Do you hear me, God? I give up."

"Finally."

Wet leaves cushioned his sudden descent, while the jarring impact was enough to knock the ball of his upper arm back into its socket. Panting from the pain and shock of falling 15 feet, Damian propped himself up on his newly hinged shoulder and surveyed his surroundings. The bushes near his head started to vibrate. Damian decided waiting around to see what walked, jumped or slinked out would only make this night worse.

Unsure of how the crash had affected his old football injury, Damian was slow getting to his feet. His first steps sent him tumbling head first into the tree. The irony of his current situation crashed down on him. Hopelessness settled deep in his gut. Damian doubled over with bouts of hysterical laughter.

"This damn tree," Damian chokes out between eruptions, "is either gonna kill me or deliver me. Oh God, what am I doing?" he asked himself.

"Is this a question you wish Abba to answer?"

Damian was struck dumb by the men in white. Seconds stretched into minutes as the robed figures waited for Damian's eyes to translate to his brain and limbs the vision before him.

"It's you!" Damian proclaimed, dropping to his knees, unfazed by the searing pain that shot up through his hip. He pulled his hands in close to his ears, unwittingly causing a canopy of leaves to gather over his head and shoulders.

"What is the obsession these humans have with hiding themselves in foliage, Brother?" Maveth asks, genuinely confused.

"We have a million life times to debate human cloaking patterns. The sooner we complete our mission, the sooner we can go home."

"But, does he understand that we can still see him?"

"Maveth, please, stay on task."

Damian snuck a peak from his stooped position, not believing what he was seeing.

"But he is not even naked, what is the point?"

"Why do you think your eyes deceive you Damian? We are indeed real." Racham reassured.

"Arise!." Maveth thunders.

"Are we not all merely servants of The Most High?" Racham interjected, attempting to ease Damians fear. "There is no need to bow before us."

Reluctantly, Damian unfurled himself from his submissive position. "Did I die?"

"That is up to you, human."

Racham motioned for Maveth to relax before speaking to their charge. "What my brother means, Damian, is that you still have the power to use the gift that our Father has given to you. You choose this night whether you will live, or whether you will die."

"I don't understand. What choices do I have? It's over for me. It's all over the news, the police are after me. No matter what I do, I lose."

"Have we spent generations on this planet for this stupidity? I will never understand what He sees in them." Fire ignited behind Maveth's eyes. "'No matter what I do I lose'," Maveth mocked. "Have you no understanding of your position in the Kingdom?"

"No." Damian admitted and felt twin boulders drop from his shoulders.

"Confession has that effect on you humans. It is an old cliché, and one that I find enormously annoying. The truth does indeed set you free. You would do well to remember that as we walk with you this evening." Maveth clutched the hilt of his sword for emphasis.

His threat sufficiently telegraphed, Maveth stepped closer to Damian, letting his flames briefly intensify before turning them down to flickers. He chuckled and slapped Damian good naturedly on his back.

"Do not worry human. We have a mission to complete. I am Maveth and this is my brother Racham. We have traveled a long way to see you through this journey. I would not bring down the Father's wrath by ending you...prematurely."

"I guess that's good to know."

"Come," says Racham, "the hour grows near."

| 63 |

"Where are we?"

"Have you never seen a crossroads human?"

"I know where we are literally. What I mean is where are we physically?"

"Where we are is not what is important Damian." Racham explained. "Where you go, from where we are, is."

"You have two choices, human. The path to your right will provide you escape from everything you're running from. You'll have a new life and a new identity. No one will know who you are or what you have done. Damian Hardwin will cease to exist."

"The path to your left will take you back home. The chips will fall where they may. I cannot say for certain that you will not be persecuted and that you will not endure any suffering for the choices you have made." Racham continued.

"Ok, so, what's the catch?"

"The catch?"

"It can't be that easy."

"Why not? It is a choice the Father has put before your kind since the beginning of time Damian."

"We have watched you over the years, human. Constantly questioning and wondering who you are and why you are here."

"The time has come for you to stop questioning."

"Choose ye this day human."

"Your life?" began Racham.

"Or His death?" Maveth finished.

THE END

Kalimah Williams was born in 1974, a little girl surrounded by a big family, in the small town of Salisbury, NC. She got to spread her wings as an Army Veteran with tours in Taegu, Korea; Bagram, Afghanistan and Washington, DC. She now resides in Raleigh, NC where her dream is to write full-time in scenic locations that include passport stamps, cultural eats and good wine. She is also the owner of PPW Publications. A company she named after her true loves: the Prophets(Micah, Nehemiah, Isaiah) Princess(Daisy) & Warrior(Kai).

CPSIA information can be obtained
at www.ICGtesting.com
Printed in the USA
FSHW010201190421
80548FS